TABLE FOR TWO

TABLE FOR TWO

KAREN SANDLER

Thorndike Press • Chivers Press
Waterville, Maine USA Bath, England

This Large Print edition is published by Thorndike Press, USA and by Chivers Press, England.

Published in 2003 in the U.S. by arrangement with Karen Sandler.

Published in 2003 in the U.K. by arrangement with the author.

U.S. Hardcover 0-7862-4528-X (Romance Series)
U.K. Hardcover 0-7540-8884-7   (Chivers Large Print)

The text of this Large Print edition is unabridged.
Other aspects of the book may vary from the original edition.

Set in 16 pt. Plantin.

Printed in the United States on permanent paper.

British Library Cataloguing-in-Publication Data available

Library of Congress Cataloging-in-Publication Data

Sandler, Karen.
    Table for two / Karen Sandler.
      p. cm.
    ISBN 0-7862-4528-X (lg. print : hc : alk. paper)
    1. Women public relations personnel — Fiction.
2. Restaurateurs — Fiction.   3. Large type books.
I. Title.
PS3619.A54 T33 2003
  813′.6—dc21   2002026615

TABLE FOR TWO

Chapter 1

"Rachel!"

Rachel Reeves hunched over her sewing machine, pressing the floor pedal harder. The motor's growl dampened, but didn't quite drown out, her stepsister Beulah's imperious command.

"Rachel!"

Her stepsister Bonnie had picked up the call, shouting up the twist of stairs to Rachel's sewing room. Their voices echoed off the walls of the rambling Indiana farmhouse and battered insistently at Rachel's ears. Narrowing her focus on the rapid bite of needle into fabric, Rachel nudged her machine into top speed.

"Rachel!"

The last impatient cry coincided with the end of the bobbin thread and Rachel could have wept with frustration. She'd have to refill the bobbin before she continued, and her

7

idleness gave her stepsisters the opportunity to interrupt with whatever craziness they were up to this time.

Not that Rachel didn't revel in the liveliness of her two drop-dead-gorgeous stepsisters. After all, if Rachel's life had to be dull as soapsuds, at least she could be entertained by sitting on the sidelines of her stepsisters' adventures. But lately, a strange restlessness had overtaken Rachel, and being a bystander to excitement had begun to lose its appeal.

"There you are," Beulah gasped out, her rich auburn hair appealingly mussed by the run up the stairs.

"As if I'd be anywhere else," Rachel muttered. The flash of hurt in Beulah's eyes made Rachel regret the uncharacteristic bitterness in her voice. She flashed her stepsister a smile. "What's up, Sis?"

Beulah fluttered an impatient hand at Bonnie as she hurried into the sun-washed sewing room. "Show her," Beulah ordered her younger sister.

Bonnie slapped a square of newspaper on the sewing machine cabinet. "Pancakes, Rachel," she said, gesturing at the clipped article. "We need pancakes."

Since Beulah and Bonnie rarely made sense on first hearing, Rachel turned her

8

attention to the newspaper clipping for clarification. Her eyes scanned the fuzzy photograph topping the scrap of paper first, stopping on the face of the man standing off to the side in the picture.

Jack Hanford, CEO of Hanford House of Pancakes, she read from the photo's caption.

Rachel ran a finger tip across the man's arresting face, wishing the picture were sharper and in color. His hair was dark — black or brown? — and his eyes light, definitely blue. She had the urge to hold the bit of newsprint up and at an angle, so that the man in the picture would look at her.

"Well?" Beulah pressed, flapping a hand at the clipping.

"What? Oh!" Rachel held the article closer, skimming the text quickly, then located the part that no doubt had her stepsisters in a tizzy:

"Do you love pancakes? Do you have what it takes to sell the fastest-growing family restaurant chain in the tristate area? Then Hanford House of Pancakes wants YOU as their spokeswoman! Come show us your stuff April 12th, 2 P.M. at Town Hall."

"That's today," Rachel said, rubbing a hand over her forehead.

Beulah gripped Rachel's shoulder, brimming with excitement. "It's our big chance!"

"Our golden opportunity!" Bonnie chimed in.

Rachel shook her head with a sigh. When the Egg Commission sought a representative for their local television spots, Beulah and Bonnie demanded egg costumes, complete with baby chicks trailing along on ribbon leashes. The ribbons tangled around Bonnie's ankles and she stumbled into Beulah, who tumbled into the lap of the chairman of the Egg Commission.

"I suppose you want pancake costumes," Rachel said, wishing her lack of enthusiasm would dissuade her stepsisters.

"Yes!" Beulah exclaimed, undeterred. "With a big pat of butter right here." She swatted Bonnie's midsection, nearly doubling her sister over.

"And a dollop of syrup here," Bonnie added, planting a fist in the middle of Beulah's back.

They'd be at each other's throats in another minute. Rachel wondered again when these twenty-something children would ever grow up. Their frequent bickering made her feel positively ancient at thirty, as if she were their mother instead of older sister.

As a ten-year-old, Rachel had fallen in love with two-year-old Bonnie and three-year-old Beulah when her stepmother had first introduced them. And when a car accident claimed both their parents five years ago, Rachel was glad for the company of her sisters. They agreed then they would stay together until Beulah and Bonnie finished college and were on their own.

Rachel never really minded that in five years her stepsisters had completed only a handful of classes, that they flitted from one part-time job to another. But at times like this, pushed to the edge of irritation by their wheedling and nagging, she'd just as soon chuck them both out of the house.

"It's nearly ten already," Rachel said, interrupting her uncharitable thoughts. "I haven't the time to make costumes."

Beulah turned puppy-dog eyes on her, wide and brown. "Oh, Rachel, you can do it. You can do anything." Beulah batted her eyelashes. "Please?"

"Please, please, please," Bonnie tossed in.

"We'll never ask you for anything again," Beulah declared.

"Never," Bonnie said solemnly, crossing her heart with an exaggerated X.

Never again today, maybe. With a sigh, Rachel gazed down again at the scrap of paper in her hand. What would it be like, she wondered, for a prince like Jack Hanford to sweep her away from all this?

Putting aside her fanciful thoughts, Rachel said to her stepsisters, "Bring down those fifties poodle skirts I made you last Halloween. I'll take off the poodles and sew on a few pancakes."

"You're a doll," Beulah said, bending from her statuesque height to give Rachel a kiss.

"A sweetheart," Bonnie chimed in, nearly squeezing the breath from Rachel with her affectionate hug.

"But I won't go with you this time," Rachel added sternly. "The egg fiasco was quite enough, thank you."

"Whatever you say, Rach," Beulah said as the two raced for the door.

They left the clipping behind when they scurried off to find the skirts, and Rachel allowed herself a few more moments to admire Jack Hanford. She could just make out a cleft in his chin, and she imagined what it would be like to run her thumb along that slight indentation. A shiver coursed up her spine at the vivid fantasy.

Her stepsisters' footsteps clattered in the hall, nearing the sewing room again. Rachel slipped the clipping into her pocket with a smile, glad to have something new to feed her dreams.

Four hours later, Rachel was parking her pumpkin-orange Toyota in the Town Hall parking lot, Beulah and Bonnie bouncing with excitement in the backseat. She'd barely turned off the engine before her stepsisters scrambled out, gray felt skirts flouncing in the April breeze.

Rachel climbed out of the car more sedately, wondering why in the world she was here. She wanted to think it was because Beulah and Bonnie had begged her to come, but she'd learned long ago to tune out her two stepsisters when the need arose.

Admit it. Rachel, you're here to see Jack Hanford.

Okay, so she wanted just a glimpse of him to see if the reality held up to the fantasy she'd spun around his picture. She knew it wouldn't — reality had always had a tendency to let Rachel down. He would probably turn out to have warts on his nose or some other blemish that had been artfully airbrushed out of the photo.

But she had to see, she had to be certain, so Rachel trailed behind her stepsisters down Main Street toward the Town Hall. The early morning shower had kissed the air with sweetness, christened the vivid green fields of Indiana corn. She should be back in her sewing room, enjoying the spring day outside her window, not trotting along after her stepsisters.

Up ahead, the Town Hall fairly burst at the seams with people, roiled with the sound of voices. Rachel's footsteps faltered as she approached the near-riot. She hated a brouhaha — so why was she here?

Because her stepsisters had asked, she told herself.

Because he *might be here and this would be my only chance to see him,* a little voice retorted.

You're setting yourself up for disappointment, Rachel told herself as she elbowed her way through a pack of pancake-costumed blondes. She half-expected Bonnie and Beulah to kick up a fuss about that, but Beulah tossed her head at the butter-bedecked crew and sniffed, "How unoriginal."

Rachel hid a smile as she slipped into an empty seat in the back of the Town Hall. Her sisters marched up to the front of the room to take their place in a line of hopefuls registering for the audition. The stage up front was crammed with people and the photographer from the *Blue Hills Gazette* was snapping shot after shot of the varied crowd.

When Rachel caught herself straining to

14

see through the mass of people up front, she knew darn well who she was looking for. Impatient with herself, she decided she might as well seek him out. Once she'd assured herself her prince was really a frog, she could put her mind at rest.

She caught a tantalizing glimpse of two men seated behind a table on the stage. The older man popped into clear view once or twice, but his companion always seemed to be half-concealed by some bizarrely costumed body. The glint of his blue eyes teased her, a broad gray-suited shoulder winked in and out of sight. It was all Rachel could do to keep from barreling through the crowd to get a clear look at him.

Then, as if a sprinkling of fairy dust had kissed him, the crowd parted just as a sunbeam slanted from the high windows. Rachel squeezed her eyes shut a moment, then looked again. But her brain, scampering with excitement through the halls of her imagination, continued to be fooled.

He was a god. An Adonis. A miracle of masculine beauty. The sun gilded the curls of his yummy chocolate brown hair, illuminated the warm blue of his eyes. If his shoulders were any broader he'd need a warning label; if that shadowy cleft in his chin were any deeper, he'd need a license for it.

Rachel gasped against the quickening pace of her heart, shivered against the honeyed warmth that seeped into her nerves. A steaming stack of pancakes had nothing on this man; he could melt butter with just one glance of his hot blue gaze.

Against all reasoning, that gaze began moving through the crowd, past the rows of spokespancake wannabes, as if searching out Rachel in the back of the room. For a heart-stopping moment, his gaze settled on her as if no one else existed, as if he'd spent his whole life looking just for her.

Angels sang, pixies danced, Rachel surely floated six inches from her chair.

Then the next applicant blocked her view. And like the soapsuds her life resembled, her fantasy burst.

Who the hell was that woman?
Jack Hanford tried to lean past the brunette dressed like a bottle of maple syrup for another glimpse of the diminutive blonde in the back of the room. But each time he tipped his head past the maple-leaf-emblazoned costume, another body in the teeming room blocked his view.

Ah, there she was. Her chin-length honey-blonde hair skimmed her jaw, half conceal-ing her face. Her eyes seemed too light for

16

brown; hazel maybe. And out of this crowd of nutcases his father's ad had shaken loose from the trees, she was the only one dressed as a normal person.

After the garish parade of the past hour, the muted swirl of beige and cream on the woman's sweater was a soothing relief. In fact, out of all the auditioners he'd registered so far, she was the only one who might possibly fit the image of the Hanford House of Pancakes restaurant chain. And she obviously wasn't even applying.

His father's raucous laugh brought Jack's attention back to the dreary matter at hand. The leer Henry Hanford gave the redheaded twins just stepping up to the table only confirmed what Jack had suspected. His father's scheme to stage small-town auditions for a Hanford spokeswoman was only a smoke screen for his true mission — his search for wife number seven . . . or was it eight?

Jack was the progeny of number two, the only one to produce an heir, the only one to die while still married to his father. The true love of his life, his father liked to say, usually with a long, wistful sigh.

Of course, he swore the same with each new partner. Jack had learned to take that declaration with a massive grain of salt.

He'd had been treated well by all the stepmothers, though, from number three when he was a toddler, to number five — six? — who bid Jack good-bye when he headed off to college. The fact that they seemed to get younger as his father got older only increased the distance Jack placed between his stepmothers and his heart.

Of course, he kept all women well clear of his heart. As a healthy, thirty-six-year-old male, Jack liked women just fine — as friends, as occasional lovers when the need arose. But he'd gotten a first-hand view of the slippery slope of marriage and he'd just as soon keep his feet on solid ground.

His father jabbed him in the ribs. "Good possibilities here, eh, Jack?"

Jack handed a numbered ticket to each of the twins. "For the loony bin," he said into his father's ear, his voice swallowed by the cacophony in the room.

"I like 'em lively," Henry said, his grin letting Jack know exactly where his father liked his women at their liveliest. Jack didn't begrudge his father his still-active libido at age seventy-five. He just wished Henry could express his appreciation with someone his own age for a change.

"That's the last of them," Jack said, passing a ticket to the final auditioner. "How did you want to handle this?"

18

His father waved a hand at him. "I figured that was your department. You're the one with the MBA."

Jack could have cheerfully strangled his father. Henry knew damn well no graduate of Purdue University would be idiot enough to concoct a scheme like this in the first place.

Jack gritted his teeth, wondering if he'd wear them to nubbins by the end of the day. "We'll call them up ten at a time and give them a once-over."

His father grinned, rubbing his hands together with delight. "Great idea, Jack. Let's bring 'em on."

As Jack named off the first ten, his eyes drifted back to the delicate blonde. Now that the crowd had all either taken seats or found places to stand at the back and sides of the room, he could see her clearly. Her gaze locked with his so briefly he almost thought he'd imagined it, then her eyes slid away to focus on her lap.

He watched as one slim hand reached up to tuck a honey-blonde strand behind her ear, and he could swear she was trembling. A sudden sharp image of his hands on her body intruded, inciting the same tremor in her slender fingers, a tremor that would build into an earth-shattering explosion . . .

19

With a shake of his head, Jack dispersed the ill-timed fantasy. Shifting in his seat, he was glad his slacks were loose. It was a damned awkward time to react to a woman that way, especially a woman who was as far as she could be from the voluptuous types he usually favored.

Returning his attention to the ten women assembled on stage, he gave each one a cursory glance. The only one that deserved a second look was contestant number three — a man in drag. Jack toyed briefly with the idea of picking the impostor, if only to spite his father.

He gave his thumbs down to the first group and called the next ten up on stage. As he quickly dispensed with the five pancake-costumed blondes, the two bottles of maple syrup, and the remaining three in get-ups entirely inappropriate for a family restaurant, his gaze strayed to the woman seated in the back. He caught her watching him again, but this time she didn't look away.

He absently called up the next group of applicants. Pulling his gaze from the honey-blonde only long enough to reject the wacky gang of ten onstage, he let his eyes feast on her. He imagined circling the tempting slope of her narrow shoulders with his arms. His gaze skimmed her slender throat, and he wondered what her pulse would feel like under his tongue.

"Jack?" his father whispered, gesturing to the restive crowd.

He'd lost track of the audition. The last group of applicants had left the stage; he had to call the next ten up. Running a finger down the list, he named off the next set of numbers, then sought her out again.

He could swear the sun had moved just to bathe her in its golden illumination. The light picked out the color of her eyes — hazel, definitely — and turned her hair to molten gold. She was a goddess, a heroine just stepped from a fairy tale, a paragon among women.

His father's voice intruded. "Now *that's* a real possibility," Henry said in Jack's ear.

He turned to his father, expecting the old lecher to be eyeing some luscious package onstage. To Jack's horror, Henry had his gaze fixed right where Jack's had been — on the honey-blonde in the back.

"She's off-limits," Jack growled, wondering where the surge of possessiveness had come from. At his father's odd look, he added, "She's not even on the list."

Henry just grinned, then returned his speculative gaze back on the woman.

Jack elbowed his father. "What do you think of these?" He tipped his head toward the assemblage onstage.

"Whatever," Henry answered, too busy winking at the honey-blonde in the back.

When the woman smiled prettily in return, Jack had to resist the urge to haul his father offstage and back into the Lincoln waiting outside. "Next ten," Jack snapped, calling off the numbers.

While the next hopefuls trooped onstage, Henry made an idiot of himself waggling his brows at the honey-blonde in the back of the room. She kept her eyes downcast, and when she did glance furtively up onstage, Jack could swear it was him she sought out. His heart did a funny tumble in his chest, no doubt a consequence of the stage lights and too many bodies in a tight space.

A half-dozen link sausages did a little dance onstage, nearly toppling each other in the process. With a barely suppressed groan, Jack plunged his fingers through his thick brown hair. Damn, he should have kept yesterday's appointment for a cut instead of haring off to Blue Hills, Indiana for his father's latest promotional scheme.

He felt her eyes on him again and had to fight to keep his expression neutral when he linked his gaze with hers. She wasn't a beautiful woman, he realized. Her features were too delicate, her eyes too large in her face. Her blonde hair was pretty, and those hazel eyes arresting, but really, she was just passably attractive.

So why couldn't he keep his eyes off her? Maybe because everything about her suggested home and family and warm-from-the-oven cookies on a plate. He'd had precious little of that kind of maternal attention as a child; maybe that was what appealed to him in the blonde woman.

Then, she smiled. It was just a timid curving of her lips, a shy glance up at him. But in that brief moment, he saw an entirely different promise, one that had nothing to do with cookies, one that had him shifting in his chair again.

Beside him, his father fiddled with his tie and refastened the top button on his jacket. Before Jack realized what he was doing, Henry had risen from his seat with a determined look in his eye. *By God, the old buzzard's on the prowl. Damned if I'll let him have my honey-blonde!*

Without taking time to consider his mental use of the possessive, Jack shot up from his seat and planted a hand on his father's shoulder before he'd taken so much as a step from the table. "Sit," he growled, pushing down with a firm hand to reinforce his command.

Then, before his father could regroup, Jack strode across the stage, past the prancing sausages and the lone fried egg. Neatly dodging the photographer, he hurried down the stage steps and up the aisle.

"Audition's over!" he barked, his autocratic tone of voice plunging the room into near silence. "I've made my choice!"

As his words rang from the cobwebbed rafters of the Town Hall, Jack zeroed in on the captivating woman in the back of the room. His long legs eating up the last few feet between them, he leaned across the three candidates seated between her and the aisle.

Eyes wide, her lips parted in surprise, she gazed down at the hand he held out imperiously in her direction. Damn, he was shaking, made weak at the knees by this one lovely woman.

"I choose you," he told her, and her sweet hazel eyes grew even wider.

Rachel stared at the large square hand held out to her, and gulped back a frisson of excitement. "I'm not auditioning," she managed, not quite able to meet his gaze.

He just reached out farther, plucking her

24

hand from her lap and tugging her from her seat. "What's your name?" he asked.

The first jolt of contact with his palm had her stuttering, "R-Rachel Reeves." She squeezed past the three women blocking her way to the aisle and prayed she wouldn't stumble. "But I'm only here for my stepsisters."

He paused in the aisle. "You can all go home," he called out over the renewed rumble of the crowd. "I've selected Ms. Reeves as the Hanford House of Pancakes spokeswoman."

"But I haven't applied!" Rachel protested, resisting him as he towed her up the aisle.

The auditioners' loud-voiced complaints increased in volume. "Audition's over!" he called out again over the noise, and the crowd finally relented, heading for the exits.

He leaned close to her to be heard over the clatter of voices. "The position lasts two months," he said. "You'll make personal appearances at each of the twelve Hanfords in Illinois, Indiana and Ohio."

"Just a minute," Rachel said, his teasing breath in her ear sending shivers through her.

He barreled on, as if she hadn't spoken, fording the stream of departing bodies like a single-minded salmon. "You're also required to tape a one-minute television spot to be aired on local stations."

Rachel looked back despairingly at the rapidly emptying room. Beulah and Bonnie stood scrunched off to one side, pumping their fists in an exuberant show of encouragement.

"Mr. Hanford!" Rachel tried to free her hand from his, to unlock her fingers from his inexorable grip.

"Jack," he said, changing position as they reached the stage, cupping his hands over her shoulders to guide her.

"Just a minute!" she said more firmly, although her voice sounded wavering to her own ears. "I never intended to apply for the job. I can't take two months off from my business."

"Then we'll compensate you for your lost time," he said, then named a salary that nearly had her swooning. She couldn't hope to make that much sewing, if she worked around the clock.

Casting one last hopeful glance about the Town Hall, she saw that only Beulah and Bonnie remained. "Why did you let them all go?"

He marched her across the stage. "Because I've made my choice."

Heavens, it was enticing. The man beside

her went leaps and bounds beyond any paltry fantasy she might have entertained about him. If anyone had air-brushed Jack Hanford, it had been Mother Nature, gifting him with an almost unfair male beauty. Rachel wondered if she'd ever uncurl her toes in her sensible beige flats.

"But I'd be no good at it, Mr. Hanford," Rachel tried again.

"I'm Jack," he corrected. "The incorrigible old man at the table is Mr. Hanford."

The old man in question had risen, his wavy gray hair as thick as his son's, the gleam of interest in his eyes flattering. She saw a sweetheart under the lined face, in the blue eyes only slightly paler than his son's. When Rachel put her hand out in introduction, the elder Hanford pulled her into an enthusiastic hug.

"Henry Hanford," he said, then gave her a broad wink as he tipped his head toward his son.

"Dad," Jack Hanford growled in warning, glowering at his father.

Rachel didn't understand Jack's disapproval. Couldn't he see the old man was just a harmless flirt? Jack didn't need to be such a grump about it.

Then Jack's hands curved around her arms and tugged her from Henry Hanford's reach, and her fingers curled to match her toes. She could sense the breadth of him behind her, feel him towering over her. Why, if she just took one little step back, she'd be pressing against him from head to toe . . .

With a gasp of dismay, Rachel shook herself free of his grasp. She faced him, keeping her gaze centered on that inviting cleft in his chin.

"Listen, Mr. Han — Jack. I can't be your spokeswoman. I'm awful in front of crowds. I get the shakes, I tip over my trongue —" She closed her eyes, took a breath and tried again. "Please," she finished softly.

And looked into his eyes, which she'd told herself would be a big mistake. Because that tempting cleft had nothing on the depths of his brilliant blue eyes. If eyes were a window to the soul, Jack Hanford's baby-blues were a wide-screen Technicolor satellite feed to his.

"Oh, please," she murmured again, although this time she wasn't quite sure what she was asking.

Jack stepped closer, one hand raised. She thought he would touch her, almost felt his finger tips graze her cheek, then his hand fell again.

He shoved his hands into his pocket. "You'll want to read the contract," he said.

Rachel shrugged. "I'm not very good at understanding those things."

He smiled and Rachel's heart lurched. "Who is? I can have our attorney explain it, or you can have your own take a look at it."

Another hitch of her shoulders. She felt like a two-year-old being asked if she wanted chocolate or vanilla. "I'm sure it's fair."

His gaze had drifted to her mouth, distracting her from something very important tapping at her brain. "Then I'll get it from the car and we can sign it right here."

"Of course," she said, still trying to figure out just what the warning bells in her mind signaled.

He flicked a glance at his father, at the older man's eager, friendly smile. "On second thought, just come with me. We'll sign the contract in the Lincoln."

"Sure," she said, and dropped her hand in the crook of his arm.

The message didn't get through as she walked out the back door of the Town Hall. It refused to come clear as they moved through the parking lot, deftly sidestepping vehicles snarled in traffic trying to turn onto Main Street. And despite the frantic bounce and click of her synapses ringing their klaxon, she never got a clue even when he ushered her into the big, black Lincoln.

It was only after, snuggled in the limousine's plush leather seats, the ink of her signature drying on the page, that she finally figured out what her wise, sensible self had been trying to say.

When the heck did she say yes?

Chapter 2

"What have I done?" Rachel moaned, her hands over her face blocking the passing scenery outside the Lincoln's windows.

"You'll be marvelous, dear," Henry Hanford assured her, patting her knee.

"What have I done?" she repeated, dropping her hands in her lap. That only made matters worse, because now she could see Jack Hanford on her right, his broad shoulders seeming to span all the space in the limousine's spacious backseat.

Shifting away from Jack, she glanced out the rear window of the Lincoln to where Beulah and Bonnie followed in Rachel's Toyota. The gears on her orange compact would be dust by the time Beulah got through driving it.

She racked her brain, trying to understand how she'd gotten herself in this predicament. She had a vague memory of

31

signing the contract, an even dimmer recall of the flash of cameras capturing hers and Jack's image in front of the Town Hall. She remembered standing next to him as the pictures were taken, wishing she could tip her head over slightly to rest it on his shoulder, to snuggle herself more tightly under the curve of his arm.

Then somehow, she ended up here, in the limo. She turned back toward the front, finally registering the flashes of green rolling past her outside the car's windows. "Why are we on the interstate?" She tapped on the glass separating them from the chauffeur. "Excuse me," she said, pointing behind her. "My house is that way."

The dark-suited man driving the Lincoln flicked a questioning glance in the rearview mirror. "Keep going, Bill," Henry said, then he smiled at Rachel. "We're headed for the Northside Mall," he told her, his hand out to pat her knee again. Jack's growl had him snatching it back with an unrepentant grin. "Have to get you outfitted."

"Outfitted?" Rachel echoed, as the Lincoln took the Evansville exit.

"Got to get you gussied up a bit," he said, his incorrigible gaze raking over her. "No offense, Miss Reeves, but your get-up's a bit . . . plain."

"She looks fine," Jack said, the rumble of his voice shivering clear to Rachel's toes.

"Fine for camouflage," Henry snorted. "If you don't mind fading into the woodwork."

"You rude old buzzard!" Jack said, turning to face his father.

Henry guffawed. "I'm only saying the lady dresses like an old maid."

Jack surged closer, his arm pressing into Rachel's as he poked a finger into Henry's chest. "One more crack like that you're riding in the trunk, Dad."

"I'm only telling the truth, son," Henry said, his smile undimmed. "Just like I always taught you."

"The truth —" Jack grabbed a handful of his father's jacket and gave him a shake. "I won't have you hurting Rachel's feelings."

Before Henry could come up with a reply to rouse his son's ire even further, Rachel's peacemaker personality came to the fore. Wrapping her hands around Jack's wrist, she tugged him back from his father, trying to ignore the heat the contact generated from finger tips to toes.

Rachel took a shaky breath, a mix of relief and loss lancing through her when Jack backed away. "He isn't hurting my feelings, honestly," she told him. "After all, it *is* just the truth."

Jack's gaze narrowed on her. "Is it?" he asked softly, sending a thrill dancing down her spine.

She pulled her gaze away, and focused on her hands twisting in her lap. "Of course. I'm dull as dishwater. I faced that fact long ago."

When she glanced at him sidelong, she saw the blue of his eyes had darkened. "And who might have convinced you of that, Rachel Reeves?"

"No one," she told him. "I mean, no one had to. When you've got stepsisters as gorgeous as mine, all it takes is one look into the mirror to get the message."

She turned to him, lifting her chin with as much pride as she could muster. "Not every woman has to be beautiful, Mr. Hanford."

"Jack," he said absently, then his finger tip touched her lightly on her chin, "But tell me, Rachel. Just what mirror have you been looking into?"

She opened her mouth, struggling for an answer. "An honest one," she said finally, but his cocked brow told her he didn't believe her.

Was he implying her looks compared with her sisters'? She nearly laughed out loud at the notion, then pushed it aside as too preposterous to consider.

She settled back in the soft seats of the Lincoln, determined to enjoy its smooth ride as it sailed down the highway toward Evansville. Behind them, the Toyota followed gamely, although she could imagine its engine gasping to keep up with the bigger car.

She sensed Jack's intense gaze on her, but she didn't dare look his way. Instead, she let her eyes drift shut, as if the rhythm of the car had lulled her into sleep. But she could have slept more easily in the midst of a blaring symphony than elbow-to-elbow with Jack Hanford.

Finally, they reached the Northside Mall exit and the Lincoln eased to a stop at the stoplight. She heard the screech of brakes behind them as Beulah careened toward the rear of the limo.

Having driven with Beulah before, Rachel didn't even flinch. To his credit, the dark-suited chauffeur only hunched his shoulders as the Toyota shuddered to a stop millimeters from the Lincoln's bumper. Then he heaved a discreet breath of relief and serenely turned the big car left on the green arrow. Beulah must have stalled Rachel's four-door, because she barely made the yellow light.

The Lincoln glided into the busy parking

lot, then pulled into an empty spot, its length taking up two spaces. Two slots over, Beulah just missed nicking the bumper of a pickup as she parked the Toyota.

The chauffeur leapt from the Lincoln's front seat and circled the car to open the door. Jack exited first, then put out a hand to help Rachel out. The apple in Eden had nothing on the temptation of Jack's broad hand.

Rachel slid her fingers across his palm, her breath catching in her throat when he closed his hand over hers. He tugged her gently, bringing her to his side. When Henry scrambled out after her, Jack pulled her closer and rested an arm lightly over her shoulders.

She tipped her head up to look at him, tried to understand the secrets in his eyes. But then Bonnie and Beulah swept up to them, their exuberance diverting her.

"Are we going shopping?" Beulah asked, her skirt swirling around her knee.

"That's right, girls," Henry said, tossing an arm around Beulah's and Bonnie's shoulders. "We're gonna get your sister some new duds."

"About time," Beulah said, rolling her eyes heavenward. "I've been begging her for years to throw away those old rags."

36

Rachel had to laugh. Beulah had never said any such thing.

Bonnie gazed up at Henry, a coquettish expression on her face. "I *love* new clothes."

"Then we'll have to see about getting you some, too," Henry said.

"And me?" Beulah asked, tossing her auburn ponytail.

"Of course, dear," Henry promised as he headed off toward the mall entrance. "Coming, son?" he called out over his shoulder.

Jack watched them go, wanting to be angry with his father, but his fondness for the old man washed away his ire. Shaking his head, he turned to his father's chauffeur. "We'll be a couple of hours, Bill, if you want to take off."

The man tipped his hat to Jack, then climbed back into the car. Beside him, Rachel watched her retreating stepsisters, her teeth worrying her lower lip.

"He isn't . . ." she said. "I mean, he wouldn't . . ." Her eyes flashed up at Jack. "They're only twenty-two and twenty-three!"

Jack settled his hand into the small of her back, and guided her toward the towering facade of the Northside Mall. "He's quite incorrigible, but I think his cut-off point is thirty. Your sisters are safe."

He could feel her resistance to the pressure of his hand and he fought the impulse to curve his fingers around her waist, to soothe her into compliance. "I'm afraid my father has never learned to act like a grown-up," Jack told her as they reached the mall's glass entrance doors.

He opened the door for her and stepped aside, catching a light fragrance in her soft blonde hair as she passed him. He wanted to bury his face in her hair, to feel its silkiness slide against his face, to breathe in her scent.

"Are you coming?" she asked, and he realized he was standing there like an idiot, the door still propped open in his hand.

"Yes. Of course."

He slipped inside and forced himself to walk beside her without touching her. She stood straight as a finishing school graduate as she moved, her soft beige skirt fluttering around her knees, her hips swaying gently. He wondered if he could span her slender waist with his hands.

"I have a similar problem with Beulah and Bonnie," she said, jarring him from his perusal of her.

He scrambled a moment to understand her, then he picked up the thread of the conversation again. "Your sisters are young. They're entitled to a little immaturity," Jack said. He allowed himself a brief touch at her waist to indicate a turn to the right. "My father has no excuse."

She went up on tiptoe and he followed her line of sight as his father and her stepsisters wove through the crowd ahead. "He's not married?" she asked, settling back on her feet.

"Not currently," Jack muttered. "You live with your stepsisters?"

She nodded. "When my dad and step-mom died, we all decided to stay in the family house." She sidestepped a stroller and gently bumped into him. "Sorry," she said.

"No problem," he said, his heart hammering in his chest, his hip tingling where she'd brushed against him. Lord, he was acting like a teenager!

"I never knew my mother," she offered, her gaze still on the group of three well ahead of them. "She died when I was a baby." She looked up at him. "How about you?"

"How about me, what?" he asked, avoiding the question.

Her hand brushed the sleeve of his jacket. "Is your mother still —"

He pulled away from her touch. "She's dead."

He shoved his hands into his pockets, keeping his gaze on the storefronts as they passed them instead of on Rachel's inquisitive face. Just as they crossed in front of a small, exclusive shop, a shimmer of blue caught his eye. He stopped, retracing his steps to get a better look at the store window.

He let out a long puff of air at the glittering confection of cobalt blue draped on the faceless mannequin in the window. Sequins and beads covered the low-cut crisscrossed bodice of the dress, trailing onto the skirt in the tantalizing swirl of a spiral. The chiffon skirt flared from a fitted waist to well above the knee. The underskirt was a mere scrap of material, just enough for modesty's sake.

He had to see this dress on Rachel. He could picture the glittering blue against her pale skin, the nipped-in waist sculpting her body. His mouth went dry as his overzealous mind added details to the image — the shadow of her breasts at the bottom of the vee, the hint of her thigh seen and unseen as the skirt fluttered around her hips. He imagined tracing the line of her leg in silky hose, lifting the hem of the skirt . . .

"We've lost them, Rachel said, dragging

his attention from the window. She stood on tiptoes again, peering up the crowded walkway.

"I want you to try this on," he said, his throat still tight from his rampant fantasy.

"Try what on?" she asked, moving to take a look. Her eyes grew round. "Oh," she said.

"It'll look like dynamite on you."

She shook her head. "I can't wear it."

"Why not?" He turned her, positioning her in front of the window to one side of the display. His gaze raked her. "It looks like your size."

"It is," she said softly. "But you can't buy it for me."

"Why not? I'm expecting we'll have some formal occasions on the tour when you'd need a dress like that."

Of course something a bit more modest would suit just as well, but he wasn't about to tell her that. She shook her head again, adamant.

"Then tell me why," he said.

Color rose in her cheeks. "Because it's mine," she said in a small voice.

"Yours?" he asked, confused.

"I made it," she clarified.

He looked from the glorious, sexy gown to Rachel in her plain, drab clothes, "You make dresses?" he asked her.

"I told you I have a small business." She shrugged. "I'm a seamstress."

"A seamstress," he said, looking again at the intricate swirl of sequins and beads on the dress. "That looks like more than something your average seamstress would create. Is it your own design?"

She squirmed, as if embarrassed to admit her talent. "I kind of make them up."

"Make them up," he repeated, then gave her a wry smile. "You come up with something gorgeous in your mind, then you put it together with your hands. That's quite a gift."

"It's no big deal," she said, backing away. "I think I see them," she told him, then hurried off down the walkway.

He followed, his longer legs quickly catching up to her. He didn't understand her self-effacing attitude toward her work, when she was obviously a genius at it. He wanted to ask her about it, ask her how long she'd been designing and sewing dresses. But most of all, he wanted to see her in the blue creation on display in the shop window.

She called out to her sisters, waving her arm to get their attention. In another moment, they were at her side, sweeping her along with them toward the upscale department store at the far end of the mall.

His father hung back to walk with him. "She's quite a peach, isn't she?"

"Beulah or Bonnie?" Jack asked.

"They're babies," his father said. "I mean Rachel."

A burning started in Jack's gut. "She's too young for you, too."

"She's thirty," Henry said. "That's old enough."

The burning spread to a full-fledged ache. "I thought you'd sworn off marriage."

"Rachel could change my mind," his father said. "Speaking of which, I've been thinking."

"What?" Jack growled.

"You've hated the idea of this tour from the get-go," Henry said with a casual flap of his hand. "Why don't you stay in the home office like you wanted? I'll take Rachel on the tour."

"No," Jack said. He'd be damned if he'd let his father get his hands on Rachel.

"But you know it'll be hard getting your work done on the road," Henry said. "I'm just a figurehead. No one needs me at the office. I'd be glad to take your —"

"I said *no*," Jake snarled. "I'm going on the damn tour."

His father smiled, far too pleased for Jack's peace of mind. "Fine, I'll stay home. You take the tour."

"Fine," Jack said, feeling neatly boxed in. But what the hell could he do? All that time alone with Henry, and Rachel would be wife number seven before the two months were up.

He couldn't bear the thought of Rachel as his stepmother. Because of her age, he assured himself, because his father ought to marry someone in their fifties or sixties. It had nothing to do with what he felt for Rachel himself. That was nothing more than mild interest.

But when they caught up with Rachel and her sisters, the hammering of his heart put paid to that lie. Okay, he felt more than mild interest in the sweet-faced blonde, but his main concern was keeping his father from wedding another youngster.

"Aren't these great," Beulah exclaimed, holding up a handful of laden hangers. She waved the collection of dresses and skirts at Jack, the soft fabric a whirl of color.

"But Rachel won't try them on," Bonnie complained, giving her sister a pout.

Pink rose in Rachel's cheeks. "They're simply not suitable for me."

"Then I think it's time you wore something unsuitable," Jack said, taking the hangers from Beulah. One hand on Rachel's shoulder, he directed her toward the fitting rooms.

"Those colors are too bright," Rachel said as she dodged a racing preschooler.

Her hair brushed Jack's hand, the feel of it tempting him to twist a curl of it around his finger. "We'll see."

"My looks are nondescript enough in neutral clothes," she said. "I'll disappear entirely in something that gaudy."

Jack gazed down at her as they took a place in the fitting room line. Was she fishing for a compliment? After what she'd said in the car, he didn't think so. She truly saw herself as plain.

And no doubt would deny any effort on his part to convince her otherwise. So he simply repeated, "We'll see," and held the hangers out to Rachel when it came her turn for a room.

She took the numbered tag from the attendant, then closed herself in the first cubicle. Jack itched to take a peek at Rachel over the door, but one look at the matron standing guard at the fitting room entrance was enough to bring him to his senses.

Instead, he turned to lean against the wall and gaze out at the store. Henry had taken Rachel's stepsisters over to the perfume counter and Jack heard their laughter and exclamations as they tried out samples of the scents. He wondered what perfume Rachel wore and where she placed it on her body — behind her ears, at her wrists, on her breasts . . .

Jack scrubbed at his face with his hands, wiping away his straying thoughts. "Rachel," he called out, wondering what was taking her so long. "I want to see."

A pause, and then she answered, "I don't think so," her voice very small.

"Show me," Jack insisted, before she could take the clothes off and put her drab camouflage back on.

"I can't," she moaned, "I look terrible."

"I don't believe you," he said. "Show me."

Another pause, then he heard the rattle of the door lock. The door swung open slowly and he saw Rachel's slender hand slip around the edge of it.

"Promise me you won't laugh," she said, her fingers gripping the door.

"Why in the world would I —"

The last word caught in his throat as she edged past the door and stepped out of the fitting room. Stunned, he gaped at her, at the rich emerald of her silk shirt, at the vivid wash of green and purple and royal blue in her skirt.

She was glorious, the soft blonde of her

hair taking on a golden sheen in contrast to the brilliant color of her shirt, her pale skin turning creamy against the emerald. The skirt draped her hips lovingly, brushing her legs just below the knees so that Jack wanted nothing more than to skim his fingers along the hem, to explore what lay hidden.

Jack dragged in a long breath, trying to slow his hammering heart. Was this the same pretty woman he had first seen in the back of the Town Hall? The one he'd considered as passably attractive? Standing there in brilliant green and purple, there was nothing passable about her.

Rachel Reeves was a knockout.

Rachel took one look at Jack's stunned expression and wanted to disappear.

"It's awful, isn't it?" she said, her voice barely above a whisper.

His gaze flew to her face. "No, absolutely not," he said, but she could hear the falseness in his assurance. "You look gorgeous."

Oh, sure, she thought, compressing her lips. "Gorgeous," she repeated, recognizing the courtesy behind his compliment, then turning to go back to the cubicle. "Well, this is a definite no."

"No!" he cried, just as she reached the door. She turned to look back at him. "I mean yes. It's a yes," he said. "We'll take it."

He couldn't be serious! Rachel searched his face, trying to figure out what he really thought. His expression puzzled her — he looked worried, confused and annoyed all at once. As if he saw something in her he didn't want to see.

His intensity made her edgy, and she flicked her tongue out to wet her dry lips. His vivid blue gaze caught the motion, dropping to her mouth, following the nervous gesture. An outrageous impulse surged through her — to cup his face with her hands, to run the tip of her tongue over his lips, to taste him.

Heat rising in her face, Rachel spun on her heel and headed back to the small fitting room. "I'll try on the next one," she gasped out, then shut the door after her.

Once safely out of sight, she brought her hands up to her cheeks, pressing her palms against them. Heavens, what was the matter with her? When had her imagination taken such a scandalous turn?

It must be a delayed consequence of turning thirty. All that sexual energy bubbling up, reminding her that she was far too old to still be a virgin. Jack Hanford was just a handy focus for her overwrought, sensually deprived libido.

She took a quick peek at him over the cubicle door. He'd turned away, she noted with relief, and stood gazing out at the vast department store. Thank goodness he couldn't read her thoughts, or she'd be even more mortified than she was already.

With shaking hands, she unbuttoned the emerald silk blouse and eased it off her shoulders. The slip of silk across her oversensitized skin threatened to conjure up more fanciful thoughts, but she squelched them ruthlessly. The silk might feel wonderful against her skin, the skirt delightful swirling around her knees, but neither were really appropriate attire for her.

With a sigh, she pulled on the next outfit, a slightly more sedate coral silk shirt and skirt. They would be more to her taste were it not for the riotous bird of paradise pattern on the skirt. The swath of green, orange and blue made her think of the tropics and sunny beaches, entirely impractical for a down-to-earth Midwestern girl.

She crept out of the fitting room stall, half-hoping Jack had abandoned his post. But he must have been listening for the rattle of the door lock, because he was watching for her when she stepped out. His face softened when he saw her, his gaze skimming the line of the skirt and blouse, his expression approving.

"Definite yes," he murmured.

"But —"

He gave her a little wave to usher her back into the fitting room. "Next," he said.

Rachel scowled at him as she returned to the cubicle. She threw on the buttery yellow sundress next, then the crimson power suit and the turquoise and black shirtdress, modeling each one for Jack. He said yes to all three — then handed her another half-dozen outfits selected by her sisters. Before Rachel could object, he'd spun her around and marched her to the fitting room.

The teal-green jumpsuit was the last straw. He said yes before he'd barely gotten a glimpse of her.

Rachel dug in her heels. "No."

"I say we take it," he said in a no-nonsense tone of voice.

"You can't make me," she said, feeling like a spoiled child.

Jack sighed. "I'm your employer now," he said to her as if she were the three-year-old she was acting like. "Leave it to me to decide what's best for you."

He all but patted her on the head. She took a calming breath. "I'm thirty years old, Jack. I think I know what I like and don't like."

"What you like isn't the issue," he said. "Only what I choose for you."

"I don't want you choosing for me!" she exclaimed.

"Then consider it a work uniform," he said, implacable. "Employer provided," Then when she might have protested further, he added, "And absolutely required."

Gnashing her teeth, Rachel stomped back to the fitting room. She stewed as she re-hung the jumpsuit. Yes, the clothes Jack had picked were in colors she'd always secretly wished she could wear, but she'd accepted a long time ago that muted tones suited her best. How dare he claim to know better what was right for her!

She turned away from the now towering stack of clothes and crossed her arms over her middle. She'd always been one to go along to make others happy, but Jack's imperious manner lit a recalcitrant spark in her. She burned to do something, anything, to defy him.

Frowning at herself in the mirror, her gaze roamed the tiny room. As she scanned the floor, a flash of bilious lime green caught her eye. Shoved under the small corner bench, the shiny vinyl dress had obviously been discarded by a customer who'd come to her senses after trying it on.

51

Rachel stooped to retrieve the dress, suppressing a shudder at the lurid color. She checked the tag for the size; it would fit, although she'd probably need a shoehorn to get it on.

Did she dare? The color would probably make her look like an escapee from a mortuary, but it might be worth it just to see the look on Jack's face. Resolute, she tugged down the side zipper and squirmed into the vinyl prison.

As she inched the confining dress around her hips, she realized she'd have to take off her bra so that it wouldn't show through the dress's halter top. She tossed her serviceable white bra aside, then snapped the halter strap behind her neck. One more wrench of the hem and the dress was in place.

Rachel attempted a deep breath, but her lungs didn't have the room to expand. The dress fit like a glove — at least one that had been left out all winter and shrunk two sizes. It mashed her breasts so that they mounded together in the keyhole front of the halter. The back shaped her rear, giving it barely legal coverage.

She had the dress on; did she have the nerve to show it to Jack? Of course she did, she told herself, moving penguin-style to the door of the cubicle. Anything to wipe that high-handed look from Jack's face.

Opening the door, she minced out of the fitting room and planted herself in front of Jack, "Well, what do you think of this one?" she asked, thrusting her chest out at him.

A tactical error, she realized when his eyes strayed to her artificially enhanced cleavage. To his credit, he dragged his gaze back up to her face.

"Ah, it's . . ." He looked the dress over, from the thigh-high hem to the keyhole front. "Interesting," he choked out.

"I like it," Rachel blurted, then wanted to swallow the words back. How could she have said such a thing?

Jack's eyes widened. "You do?" He seemed to be struggling to keep a straight face.

Stubborn, Rachel turned to the three-way mirror and viewed herself again. The mirror's multiple reflections revealed even greater sins. The waist bit into her skin and the luminous green reflected against her face, giving her a fishy pallor.

"Yes," she insisted. "In fact, I'd say I like this one best."

"Okay," he said slowly. "We'll get it then."

Rachel gave him a curt nod, then crab-walked back into the fitting room. Escaping from the dress was a dicey thing; for a panicked moment she thought she'd have to call the attendant for assistance. But finally, she peeled the thing from her, tossing it aside as if it were a snake.

She kicked it back under the bench, breathing hard. She'd just leave it there, pretend she'd forgotten it. No way would she actually buy the thing.

Staggering under the massive weight of clothes, she edged out of the fitting room. Jack quickly took the hangers from her, handing several of them off to his father and her stepsisters. He left her with a manageable few that she draped over her arm.

"That's all of them then?" he asked.

"Yes," she said with a lift of her chin. "Every one of your choices."

With a ghost of a smile, he guided her toward the nearby cash register with a light touch of her fingers. They hadn't gone ten paces before the woman from the fitting room came hurrying after them.

"You forgot this one!" she called out, the hideous green dress flashing in her hand.

The clerk caught up with them and laid the vinyl monstrosity on top of Rachel's stack. "You looked so marvelous in it," the woman said, "I knew you wouldn't want to leave it behind."

Rachel opened her mouth, intending to

tell the woman she'd changed her mind. Then she caught a glimpse of Jack's knowing grin, the gleam in his eye. No way would she back down now!

She smiled politely at the woman. "Thank you."

Spine straight, Rachel continued to the checkout stand and placed her pile of clothes on the counter. Her sisters followed, exchanging glances as they eyed the green dress. Rachel kept her chin up and her mouth shut as the cashier totaled up the purchase.

The final amount had Rachel gasping, although Jack whipped out his Gold Card without breaking a sweat. He scrawled his signature on the receipt, then parceled out the bags and boxes to his father and the three women. He left one hand free to place on Rachel's shoulder, his fingers making light contact as they returned to the limo.

As Bill loaded their purchases in the trunk, Henry turned to Rachel. "You don't mind taking my son over to his hotel, do you? I promised your sisters a ride in the limo."

The thought of sharing the small space of her Toyota with Jack set off alarms inside her, but she couldn't think of a reasonable excuse to say no. "I guess not," she said, glancing at Jack. His brows were drawn together in suspicion.

Henry opened the door for Beulah, stepping aside to let her and Bonnie enter the car. "There is one other thing, though. About the tour."

"What's that?" Jack asked, his quiet tone signaling further alarm.

Henry swung into the limo. "Just a little gimmick I set up."

"Dad," Jack said, sharp warning in his voice.

Rachel glanced up at Jack, his dark look filling her with unease. "What gimmick?"

"A publicity stunt for the tour," Henry said with a grin. "You're going to be husband and wife."

Chapter 3

The car door slammed shut before Jack could thunder out his response to his father's preposterous suggestion. "Dad!" he yelled, pounding on the closed window.

Henry wouldn't have opened the window, of that Jack was certain. But Bill wanted to keep his job. He lowered the back window using the front seat controls.

Jack slammed both hands on the open window frame. "What the hell are you talking about?"

His father's unrepentant grin didn't falter. "It'll have extra kick if Rachel's more than the spokeswoman for Hanford's. If she's your wife —"

"I'm damn well not going to marry Rachel!"

He heard her soft gasp at his elbow and spared her a quick look. She was studying her toes, color high in her cheeks.

He turned back to his father and hissed, "We're not getting married, you old goat."

Henry had the audacity to look miffed, "I never said you were. If you'd only give me a moment to finish . . ."

Jack didn't bother to remind his father that he'd been about to leave after dropping his unfinished bombshell. Instead Jack just waved an impatient hand for him to continue.

Henry slicked the side of his silver hair back with his fingers. "It'll be strictly for show. A pretend marriage, if you will."

"And why would we pretend to be married?" Jack asked.

Henry examined his neatly manicured nails. "To add some oomph to the publicity tour, to give it a little sizzle, a little sex."

Rachel's gasp was more audible this time. Jack would have given his father a poke if he weren't struggling to keep the images of sex and Rachel from tangling in his mind.

At least Henry had the grace to look chagrined. "I'm speaking figuratively, my dear. By taking on the persona of husband and wife, you snag the interest of the young married couples with children, the family values folk, the people we want to attract to our restaurants."

Jack glared at his father. "I think we can

do that without pretending to be married."

"But appearing as husband and wife will be much more effective," Henry said. "Besides, it's too late. Advertising's already in place. Or will be by tomorrow."

A lead weight clunked to the bottom of Jack's stomach. "What advertising?"

"Posters," his father said. "Life-sized stand-up pictures of you and the missus at every location."

"She's not my missus!" Jack exclaimed.

Rachel zeroed in on the rest of what his father had said. "Pictures?" she said. "What pictures?"

"The ones the photographers took this afternoon," Henry said as the window slowly rose. "So consider yourselves married, folks. For the next two months."

Jack stood stunned as the limo's engine purred to life and it glided from its parking space. "He can't do this."

Rachel kept her gaze fixed on the retreating black Lincoln. "He already has. Oh, I bet I look horrible in those pictures."

"What about your contract?" he asked her. "I don't recall any mention of marriage, pretend or otherwise."

Rachel tipped her head up at him. "I'm expected to take on 'any other appropriate roles as assigned by the corporation,'" she quoted. "I suppose that might include playing your wife."

"You *did* read the contract," Jack said.

She shrugged. "I have a photographic memory."

Jack gazed down at her, the flecks of gold in her hazel eyes sensually evocative. Why did everything about her make him think of sex? He was beginning to think he had a pornographic memory.

"You don't have to do this," he said, clamping down on his wayward thoughts.

She smiled, a sweet, shy curving of her lips. "It might be fun. I always wanted to try my hand at acting."

Most of the acts Jack contemplated with her involved being horizontal. Good Lord, when did he get such a dirty mind?

"It'll be tough," he said. "I presume my father wants our marriage to look like a happy one. We'll have to pretend we're in love."

Jack didn't understand the little lurch in the vicinity of his heart as he said the word "love," any more than he comprehended the yearning that flashed across Rachel's face. He turned away, staring out over the parking lot, hands shoved into his pockets.

"I think I could manage that," she said, softly.

Her voice sent a shudder down his spine that settled low in his groin. Why, when even a faux marriage should have sent him screaming across the parking lot, did the idea of her in love with him hold such appeal?

He turned back to her. "We'll do it, then."

Her gaze was steady on his, her eyes wide. The sun hovered just over the horizon behind them, gilding her face, throwing his shadow across her. A breeze kicked up, sending a lock of her hair over her cheek, and he reached to tuck it back behind her ear without thinking.

As soon as he touched her, he couldn't pull his hand away. He followed the curve of her ear as he secured the silk of her hair, then traced along her jaw, to her chin, up to her lower lip. He rested his thumb there, his fingers curled under her chin, and he realized it would take just a slight tug to bring her face into position to kiss her.

He had to drop his hand, *now*. Instead, he drew the pad of his thumb across her lip, enjoying its satiny texture, the slight moisture at the corners. What would it taste like, he wondered, if he followed that seam with the tip of his tongue?

She sighed, her breath caressing his hand. The gold in her eyes seemed to darken to amber and her eyelids fluttered as if they were too heavy to keep open. He imagined her eyes closing in slow pleasure as he brushed his lips across hers.

The distant honk of a horn startled him and he pulled his hand back, returned it to his pocket. She was blushing again, her head dipped down as she fumbled with her purse. The lock of hair had slipped free once more, but damned if he'd hazard touching her again.

"We'd better go," she said breathlessly. He nodded and they headed for her car.

"Are you hungry?" he asked once they were seated in the orange Toyota.

"I could eat something," she said, head turned to look out the rear as she backed from the parking space.

"We could go out," he said, "or . . ."

She flicked him a glance as she drove. "Or?"

"We could get room service at my hotel," he said.

The look she gave him spoke volumes about the lunacy of that idea. "We'll go out," she said. She pulled up to the exit of the parking lot, then headed out into the street. "What do you feel like eating?"

"Anything but pancakes," he muttered.

She laughed. "Or sausage."

He laughed with her, the humor a release from the stress of the day. He could relax so easily with her, free from the demands and expectations of other, more complex women.

Then she turned to him at a stoplight, her delectable mouth spread in a smile, her wind-tossed hair tucked appealingly behind one ear, and he realized there was nothing simple about Rachel. Watching her, he had the distinct feeling he'd just pole-vaulted from the frying pan directly into the fire.

Rachel sat back in her chair with a sigh and sipped her cooling tea. Head tipped down, she stole a glance at Jack seated across the table from her as he finished the last of his steak.

Catching her looking, he gestured with his fork. "Had enough to eat?"

"Plenty," she said, although she'd eaten barely half of her club sandwich. How could she eat when all she could think about was being in love with Jack Hanford?

Pretending to be in love, she corrected. And pretending to be married. An acting job. A role to play. Easy as pie.

Too easy.

"Steak tender?" she asked, then cringed at the inanity of her question.

"It's fine," he said, pushing his plate aside. "Can you be ready by Sunday?"

I'm ready now, she thought, then realized what he was asking. "I'll have to turn a couple of clients over to another seamstress, but I was pretty much between projects. Three days should be enough to tie up all the loose threads."

He smiled at her weak joke, then reached across the table to lay a finger against her hand curved around the teacup. He grazed the back of her hand lightly with his finger tip in a mesmerizing circle.

"Is there anything else you need?" he asked, his low voice rumbling clear to her core.

You, she thought, *touching me like that all over.* Her gaze locked with his and she was certain he knew exactly what she'd been thinking. The blue of his eyes darkened to navy and she felt a tension in him that pushed at her, teased her, until she wanted to pull him across the table toward her.

She jerked away, upsetting her tea so that the warm sweet liquid washed across her hand. "Sorry," she gasped, blotting at the table with a paper napkin. She managed to dam the spreading pool of tea, but she could feel its stickiness drying on her hand.

"Excuse me," she said, pushing back her chair.

Rachel wove through the tables of the coffee shop, heading for the women's bathroom. As she bent over the sink, letting cool water run over her hands, she stared at her image in the mirror. What she saw there — wide eyes, parted lips, mussed hair — shocked her.

Lord, she looked as if she'd been thoroughly kissed and he'd barely even touched her. Just that light, brief brush of his finger. How in the world would she stand two months in close quarters with Jack Hanford?

Dragging in a breath, she filled her cupped hands with water and wet her face. She'd never been so attracted to a man. The briefest of glances, the barest contact sent her heart rocketing in her chest. Another moment at their table and she would have melted into a puddle on the floor.

Rachel shook off her hands and tugged out a paper towel. She had to keep her head about this. Her one-sided attraction for Jack would be embarrassing if he were to discover it. He would be polite about it — a man like him must have plenty of homely types like her swooning at his feet — but it would be mortifying nonetheless.

Finger-combing her hair in a hopeless

attempt to neaten it, she strode out of the bathroom. She hadn't gotten two steps from the door when she ran into a solid, living wall.

"Oh!" she said, her hands plastered across Jack's chest.

"Sorry," he said, reaching out to steady her. "I paid the bill and thought I'd wait for you here."

His hands moved to cover hers, trapping them against his chest. She tipped her head back to look up at him and wished she hadn't. It made it far to easy to imagine him lowering his lips to hers.

He gave her hands a squeeze, then stepped back. He raked his fingers through his hair as he backed away another pace and she could swear she saw a tremor in his hands.

No doubt a reaction to their collision when she'd barreled out of the rest room. She, on the other hand, couldn't seem to stop shaking over the feel of his firm chest still burning into her palms.

"I'd like to get back to my hotel," he said, his voice rough as he gestured impatiently toward the exit. He obviously couldn't wait to get away from her.

She followed him out of the coffee shop into the cool, humid night. "This must be pretty tedious for you."

"What's that?" he asked as they reached her car. He held his hand out for her keys and she dropped them into his palm.

"Spending time with me," she said, stepping back as he opened the car door for her. She climbed into the passenger seat and waited for him to walk around.

"Why would that be tedious?" he asked as he started the engine.

"I'm not the most exciting person to be with. You must have figured that out in the first ten minutes during dinner." He'd asked her question after question about herself, and her mundane answers made her wish she could have fabricated a more scintillating persona. "I've had a very ordinary life."

"Maybe," he said, pulling out of the parking lot. He glanced her way, his expression enigmatic in the dim light, "But that doesn't make you an ordinary person."

She mulled over that for several silent moments, then decided he was too courteous to agree that she was dull as soapsuds. "Where are you staying?"

"Here in Evansville," he told her. "At the Marriott by the airport."

Her gaze fell on his hands as he drove. He gripped the steering wheel of her car exactly where she wrapped her own fingers. She'd never be able to drive her car again without thinking of his large, powerful hands wrapped around —

She shook her head to dispel her wandering thoughts, and racked her brain for small talk. "This must be like driving the pumpkin after that limo of yours."

"Pumpkin?" He shot her a baffled look.

"Like in *Cinderella*," she explained. "The fairy godmother turned a pumpkin into a beautiful coach."

He slanted her a smile. "What would that make me, then? A rat?"

"What?"

Jack grinned. "Isn't that what the fairy godmother used to make the coachman? A rat?"

Rachel had to laugh. "I thought it was a dog."

"Now that's a more flattering image," he said with a chuckle.

She gazed at him, at the slash of white of his smile, the chocolate brown hair that feathered his collar. If he was anyone in the old Cinderella tale, it was the handsome prince.

"Actually," he said, "I'm more used to cars like this than the limo. The Hanford chain didn't really take off until I was in college. It took a long time for Dad to be able to afford a new car."

Rachel smiled as she thought of the incorrigible old man. "He's a love, your father."

Jack shot her a look that flashed with anger before he returned his attention to the road. "A charmer," he said tightly.

She puzzled over that a moment, then turned to stare out the window. "I hope you don't have a girlfriend," she said, then wanted to slap the words back.

He slanted her an amused look. "Acting the jealous wife already, are you?"

"Yes, I mean, no!" She took a breath, "What I mean is, if you had a girlfriend, I thought it might be difficult to explain why you're going off with some other woman for two months." Her hand flew to her mouth as a thought occurred to her. "You're not married, are you?"

"Of course not," he said. "My dad would never have come up with such a diabolical scheme if I were already . . ."

He frowned as his voice drifted off. "He wouldn't," he said softly, fingers drumming the steering wheel.

Rachel wanted to ask what Jack's father would or wouldn't do, but they'd pulled into the Marriott parking lot. She climbed out of the passenger side of the car and crossed to the driver's side. Jack waited for her, one hand on the car door as she slipped inside.

"Call me when you get home," he said. "I want to know you've made it safely."

"Okay," she said, eyes on his tall frame backlit by the bright hotel lights.

"Rachel," he said, gaze intent. He looked away a moment, staring off into the night, then tipped his head back down to her. "Rachel," he said more softly.

She had no warning, no clue of what he intended when he bent closer to her. She thought he might have one more admonition about calling him, one last request. But then his hand curved around her cheek, pulling her face toward him and she realized he intended to kiss her.

On the cheek, she told herself, he would just kiss her on the cheek. She turned her head to offer that part of her face, but his hand tightened imperceptibly and held her in place. One hand braced on the car, he bent his tall frame down to her and brushed his lips against hers.

One touch had her gasping. When his lips returned to her mouth to linger a bit longer, she gave up breathing altogether. Her lips parted without her knowing they had, and she felt just the barest tip of his tongue graze along the open seam.

Jack's low groan shuddered deep inside her as if the sound had come from her. Then his hand fell away from her face and he straightened.

"Call me," he rasped, then he shut the door and backed away.

Rachel supposed she should be glad the engine was still running; her trembling fingers would've never been able to turn the key. As it was, she didn't know if she was capable of driving the twenty miles back to Blue Hills.

Some autonomous part of her brain must have taken over, because her hand covered the gear shift and shoved the car into first. She stalled out the car when her weak-as-water left leg slipped off the clutch before her right had located the accelerator. Miraculously, she remembered how to restart the engine, and even recalled how to drive.

Back on US-41, she did her best to hold back her scampering thoughts as they scurried to build a mountain out of the molehill of Jack's kiss. It meant nothing, she told herself, it was just a friendly kiss on the lips.

She would buy that if she could ignore the part about his tongue, sliding in briefly to taste her, to tempt her. She couldn't quite categorize that as friendly, although for the life of her, she couldn't fathom why Jack would have intended anything else.

Maybe it had been an accident. He'd meant to give her a brotherly peck, his mind had been elsewhere and his tongue just . . . slipped out. Which would explain why he'd seemed so upset afterward; he was probably embarrassed by the whole thing. No doubt he was in his hotel room right now, hoping she hadn't misconstrued his blunder.

Rachel reached Blue Hills and turned off Main Street toward her house. She'd set him straight when she called. After all, they'd be spending so much time together in the next two months, they couldn't have this awkwardness between them.

Once inside her house, she lugged the phone book up to her room and dropped it on her bed. She found the number for the Marriott and quickly dialed it on her bedside phone before she could lose her nerve.

"Hello?" His deep voice rendered her speechless for a moment.

"It's me," she said breathlessly. "Rachel."

"You made it home okay, then," he said.

She heard the tension in his tone and guessed he was still feeling uncomfortable about what had happened in the hotel parking lot. She had to put his mind at ease.

"About what happened," she said. "When I dropped you off."

A hesitation, then he said, "What about it?"

"I know when you kissed me, you didn't intend to . . ." She gulped, trying to think of a delicate way to put it. "I mean, I know it was an accident."

"There was nothing accidental about our kiss," he said, the rasp of his words feathering down her spine.

"Not the kiss itself," she said in a rush, "but the other part, when you unintentionally —"

"There was nothing unintentional about that either," he said.

Rachel squeezed her eyes shut. This wasn't going the way she expected at all. "I have to go," she said, helpless to find her way out of her confusion.

"I'll see you Sunday," he said. "You can leave a message on my voice mail if you need anything else before then."

I need you, she thought shamelessly, then scrambled for the pad by the phone when he rattled off his voice mail number. She said her good-byes, then dropped the phone back onto its cradle.

She undressed quickly and showered, then pulled on a light flannel nightgown and crawled into bed. She lay there in the dark, the silence of the house broken only by the boisterous return of her stepsisters a half-hour later. She replayed Jack's kiss over and over in her mind.

It wasn't accidental. It wasn't unintentional. And it went far beyond friendly, well into the realm of a lover's kiss.

One question tumbled over and over in her mind as sleep evaded her long into the night.

Why?

Why? Jack thought. Why the hell had he kissed her?

Because he was an idiot. Because he'd let his adolescent lack of self-control drive him instead of his better sense.

He shifted restlessly in bed and tried to forget how it had felt pressing his lips against Rachel's. How sweet that one short taste of her had been. How warm and satiny her skin had felt against his palm.

Hell, he got harder not thinking of her than he did if he just let himself remember. He punched the pillow as if it were at fault instead of his own wayward libido. But he had only himself to blame for following the urgings of the all-too-eager friend between his legs.

74

With a growl of frustration, he sprang from the bed. Pacing the length of the spacious room, he contemplated soaking himself in another cold shower. But he knew damn well it wouldn't do any good. Rachel had crept under his skin; no amount of water, no matter how icy, would wash her away.

He plunged a hand into his already rakish hair. Two months. How would he stand two months with her? She was so damned luscious he wanted to lick her from head to toe, taking his time on the particularly tasty parts. He imagined burying his face between her legs, touching her sensitive center with his tongue, driving her to ecstasy.

He groaned and slammed a fist against the wall. This had to stop. He couldn't let his imagination run wild like this. Rachel Reeves was now an employee of his; he'd be in a mountain of trouble if he took advantage of her the way his body was prompting him to.

Damn this scheme of his father's — asking them to pretend to be husband and wife. Somehow, the pretense added to the temptation, urged him to take what Rachel would offer if she were truly married to him. It was far too easy to imagine her in the role of wife, waiting for him when he returned home each day, ready for him each night in bed . . .

With another snarl of frustration, Jack strode back to the bathroom and twisted the shower knob to full cold.

Chapter 4

Jack gazed down at Rachel, snuggled in the corner of the Lincoln's expansive backseat, her chest rising and falling with the regular breathing of a deep sleep. What must have been a frantic three days for her, coupled with a late start to the first stop on their tour, had taken its toll. She'd fallen asleep the moment Bill had pulled the Lincoln onto I-64.

Jack tore his gaze from her and stared out the window. It had taken all his willpower to resist calling her between Thursday and Sunday. He'd had a myriad excuses and opportunities to do so. Rachel had left messages on his voice mail requesting information on their itinerary and contact numbers to leave with her sisters. Details had come up in his own mind that he'd had to relay to her.

But he'd forced himself to delegate all

communication with Rachel to his secretary. He'd justified the passing on of that task to Lucy because he'd had an overwhelming number of odds and ends to arrange himself before he could take off for two months. The fact that Lucy could have handled much of that minutiae as well, leaving him free to deal with Rachel personally, he didn't choose to consider.

So he had no right to censure her coolness toward him when he picked her up late Sunday afternoon for the drive to East St. Louis. After his out-of-control kiss Thursday night, his hands-off approach must have confused her, maybe even hurt her. But he'd needed the distance, the time to reconstruct the walls he used to protect himself from emotional involvement.

So it was just as well she fell asleep so quickly in the car. A wide-awake Rachel was difficult enough for him to deal with, let alone the sweet-faced angel sleeping next to him. She sighed, shifting on the seat, and he felt a tightness in his chest that had him aching to pull her close.

The Lincoln slowed and rolled into the hotel parking lot, stopping under the front canopy. Bill leapt from the driver's seat and hurried around to Jack's door.

"Get the luggage, would you, Bill?" Jack

told the chauffeur, then turned back to Rachel.

"Hey," he said softly, running a gentle finger down her arm. The vivid green silk of her sleeve seemed alive with her warmth. She stirred at his touch, then snuggled more deeply into the cushions.

"Rachel," he said a little louder, giving her shoulder a squeeze. She scrunched her face, as if unhappy with the prospect of waking, then opened her eyes.

She looked around her. "Where are we?" she murmured, a thread of sleep running though her voice.

"The hotel," he said. "We'll be staying here for the night."

Her eyes flicked to his face, a mix of fear and sensual awareness in their depths. A throbbing heat settled at the base of his spine, holding him rigid for several long moments.

"Let's go," he said, his voice rougher than he'd intended. He swung himself from the car and held out a hand to help her from it. She hesitated a moment before she slid across the seat toward him.

She dropped his hand as soon as she was on her feet. "What time is it?"

"Nearly six. We have time to relax and change before dinner."

He stepped aside, letting her precede him through the revolving door into the hotel lobby. She didn't wait for him, heading straight for Bill who stood juggling luggage and hotel keys. She smiled up at the chauffeur, as if grateful to see him.

Jack wanted to growl like a jealous dog and usher her away from the happily married Bill. He felt ashamed of his ill-placed jealousy, but not enough to keep him from stepping between the two and nudging Rachel aside.

"All set," Bill said, handing Jack the key cards for their rooms.

"And you arranged for the car tomorrow?" Jack asked him.

"They'll deliver it to the hotel by seven." The dark-haired man grinned up at Jack. "I would have been happy to drive you on the tour."

"Two months is too long to be away from that pretty young wife of yours," Jack told him, intent on letting Rachel know Bill wasn't available. "Besides, someone has to keep an eye on my father."

Bill nodded, his grin wider. "Will do." He nodded at Rachel. "Enjoy your trip, Ms. Reeves."

Bill headed back out of the lobby, leaving Jack and Rachel alone. Rachel fiddled with her purse strap, eyes downcast. "So Bill's not coming with us."

Jack's jaw tightened at the wistful note in her voice. "Sorry to disappoint you. It wouldn't be fair to him, especially with his wife expecting."

She tortured the strap with her fingers. "I just thought . . . that it would be good . . . to have someone else with us."

Her eyes flashed up to his, and he saw that trace of fear in them again. He felt like a real dog now, for instilling that uneasiness in her.

"Rachel," he said, waiting until she met his gaze. "I'm sorry. I was out of line the other night."

Her eyes widened. "You were?"

"I shouldn't have touched you," he said, squelching the urge to do just that as he gazed into the turbulent depths of her eyes. "I won't do it again."

She blinked, and he could have sworn she looked disappointed. "You won't?"

"You're my employee," he reminded her, "I shouldn't take advantage of you that way."

She smiled then, and a dimple winked in her cheek. Damn, he'd never been able to resist dimples. "We're supposed to be husband and wife, Jack," she said. "You might have to kiss me in public."

81

In public, he might have a prayer of keeping himself under control. "We'll cross that bridge when we come to it."

He turned away from her and her enchanting dimples to signal the bell captain. After giving the man their room number, he ushered Rachel to the elevators.

"What floor?" she asked, her fingers hovering over the buttons.

"Twenty-eighth," he said. "We're in the executive suite."

The wary look returned to her eyes. "Suite? As in, you and me in one suite?"

Jack raked his fingers through his hair, the reminder that they'd be sharing a room making him restless. "One suite, two bedrooms. I thought it might raise a few eyebrows if Mr. and Mrs. Hanford had separate rooms."

"Oh," she said, subjecting her purse strap to more anxious twisting. "Two bedrooms should be fine."

Only if they were in different hotels. Jack put a hand out to hold the elevator door as they arrived on their floor. Rachel sidled past him as if she didn't dare get too close. Jack again cursed his out-of-control libido that had brought her to mistrust him like this.

He glanced at the numbers posted on the wall and gestured to the right. She walked alongside him, back straight, purse held close to her side.

"Here it is," he said, pulling out the key card and shoving it into the slot. The green light flashed and he pushed open the door.

"Oh!" she said softly as she stepped inside the suite.

He followed her in and watched her as she turned, eyes wide, taking in the details of the sitting room. The lush furnishings were covered in muted gray and coral, the colors echoed in the walls and drapes. The warm tones of ash and birch accented the plusher upholstered pieces.

"Look at this," she said, running her fingers over the speckled gray granite slab topping the wet bar. Her hand caressed the brass fixtures on the sink, then she ran a finger tip across the bottles lined neatly on the shelf above.

She turned to him, her eyes bright. "It's beautiful."

He couldn't help but smile at her excitement over the luxury in the room. "Come see the bedrooms."

Her cheeks colored slightly, and he could have kicked himself at the suggestiveness of his invitation. Forcing a matter-of-fact tone to his voice he said, "Yours is this way."

The bedroom continued the color

scheme, with added touches of teal in the pillow shams and canopy over the bed. Rachel's smile of delight returned as she roamed the room, opening the cherrywood armoire that held the television and stereo, examining the fireplace, running her gaze over the well-stocked bookcase.

"Bathroom's in there," he said, pointing off to the right.

If the sitting room and bedroom were well appointed, the bathroom was downright sybaritic. Mirrors wrapped around the room, lit above the vanity area with soft lights. Pillowed limestone covered the floor and glass bricks enclosed the double shower. A tub the size of Texas, complete with spa jets, dominated the far end of the room.

Rachel's jaw dropped as she spun to take in all the details of the room. "This is incredible," she said. "I've never seen anything like it."

"It *is* nice," he said, enjoying the multiple reflections of Rachel in the mirrors.

"Nice?" She ran a hand over the thick teal and gray towels. "I've never seen this much luxury all in one place."

Her eyes were bright as she looked around her, her lips parted with the joy each detail of the room gave her. Jack felt inexplicably proud to have had a hand in her delight.

He'd always thought of money as a convenience, a vehicle to provide him the freedom he craved. But he'd never seen it as a way to indulge someone else. He'd given gifts to women before, usually jewelry just before they parted company. None of those recipients had ever shown the enthusiasm Rachel did for the extravagant room around her.

"I'm glad you like it," he said, his heart filled with the pleasure of having provided it for her.

She slanted him a look, a faint blush washing across her cheeks. "Thank you," she said, and a ridiculous joy spilled over inside him.

He stepped back from her, irritated with himself, with his overblown reaction to her enjoyment. "I'll be in my room," he told her as he turned on his heel. "Dinner at seven-thirty."

He strode across her bedroom, keeping his gaze shuttered from the frilly bed. He sliced a path through the sitting room without breaking stride and didn't pause until he'd reached his own bedroom and slammed the door behind him.

He gripped the knob, resisting the urge to wrench it from the door. Maybe the next stop they should get separate rooms and to hell with how it would look. Or maybe he

should call his dad and call off the whole insane idea.

He pushed away from the door and
dragged off his moss green polo shirt, tossing it to the floor. Two rooms wouldn't do
any damn good. And no way would he throw
Rachel to his wolf of a father. He'd gotten
himself — and her — into this and he would
see it through.

With an exasperated sigh, he shucked his
slacks and headed for the shower.

Rachel sank against the vanity with a sigh,
the sound of Jack's slamming door ringing
in her ears. Breathing deeply, she gripped
the coral-colored granite sink top, willing
herself to calm down. When she thought she
could move again without trembling, she let
go of the vanity and returned to the bedroom.

She shut the bedroom door more quietly
than Jack had, shaking the last of the tension
from her shoulders now that she had some
privacy. She'd never intended for him to see
how much she was attracted to him, but
from his anger just now, she hadn't succeeded.

He was probably angry with himself for
leading her on with his kiss, for making her
think he felt the same way. She didn't know

what had prompted him to brush her lips with his, but she was certain it wasn't any great sexual urge. Maybe he'd been without a woman for some time, or he was curious to see if kissing a plain woman would be the same as kissing a beautiful one.

It was obvious he now wanted to wash his hands of the whole affair. Her inability to hide her attraction for him only made the situation more awkward.

Gazing at herself in the mirror, she nudged a strand of hair behind her ear with a sigh. She would just have to put a sturdier lock on her emotions. She'd already spent too much time fantasizing about Jack Hanford. It wasn't his fault he'd become a featured player in so many of her dreams.

Undressing quickly, Rachel gave the decadent Jacuzzi tub a longing look, then stepped into the shower instead. As she rinsed the fragrant shampoo from her hair, she imagined her Jack Hanford–inspired wishful thinking swirling down the drain with the soap bubbles.

As she pulled on a red-fringed Western-style shirt and jeans, she told herself she'd put aside those schoolgirl fantasies she'd built around the dark-haired, blue-eyed CEO. As she blow-dried her hair, she pictured her fanciful thoughts of Jack dispersing like dust in the warm gust of air.

Then she spoiled it all when she stretched out on her bed to read. For the entire thirty minutes that she should have been engrossed in her murder mystery, her rebellious heart teamed with her willing brain, filling her daydreams with Jack's smile and Jack's kisses.

Rachel spooned up the last of her chocolate mousse, holding it on her tongue until the sinful sweetness melted away. Sitting back in her chair, she gazed around her at the brightly lit hotel restaurant. Her stomach full, her emotions reined in, she felt proud that she'd managed dinner with hardly a thought straying into forbidden territory.

Except for the time her ankle brushed the rough denim of Jack's jeans, and that moment his fingers stumbled against hers as he reached for the salt shaker, she'd kept her fantasies under control. In fact, her heart never once kicked into overdrive — except, of course, for that time when she caught his intense blue gaze fixed on her just as the waitress left with the menus. And then it had picked up its pace a bit when she'd shifted to lay her napkin on her lap, and her knee pressed briefly against his under the table.

But it had been a piece of cake to ignore the play of ropy muscles in his arms below the rolled-up sleeves of his blue chambray shirt. And when it occurred to her that the rich, smooth chocolate taste of the mousse matched the bittersweet flavor of his kiss, she didn't give it a moment's thought.

Well, maybe one moment. Or two. But she pushed aside the troublesome comparison almost as soon as it sprang into her consciousness.

So she was definitely on the road to putting her feelings for Jack in their place. Not even the tantalizing curls of golden hair snugged in the vee of the open collar of his shirt would persuade her off the straight and narrow.

Then he ruined it all.

"You have a bit of chocolate on your mouth," he said, his voice a low rumble.

Rachel groped for her napkin, wondering why such an innocent remark set her heart to stuttering. "Where?" she asked, dabbing at each corner of her mouth.

The blue of his eyes seemed to darken as they fixed on her. "Here," he said, reaching across the table.

No, no, no! cried her sensible side as his thumb grazed her lower lip. *Yes, yes, yes!* her illogical heart contradicted.

Jack rubbed, once, twice, the contact screaming along her nerve endings. When he pulled back, Rachel thought she could breathe again. But then he wet his thumb with his tongue and returned to his sensual assault.

If he hadn't lingered there a moment longer than he needed to cleanse the spot she might have had a chance. But that last mesmerizing stroke of his thumb drove all moderation from her mind, leaving her a quivering mass of need.

All from that single touch. As she raised a trembling hand to cover her mouth, she decided she needed her head examined. Many years of therapy might wake her up to the fact that she'd carried this fantasy of Jack to dangerous extremes.

"Thank you," she whispered.

"You're welcome." His eyes gleamed as he lowered his hand in his lap again. If her own brain hadn't been so addled, she would have sworn she saw a tremor in his fingers before he hid his hand away. Too much coffee at dinner, she supposed, although she could see he'd barely touched his cup.

Rachel waited until the waitress cleared away the last of their dishes before she spoke again. "We make our first appearance tomorrow?"

He nodded, his restless hands back on the table. "Just outside of East St. Louis." He sipped his coffee, wincing at the taste. "We just completed a renovation of one of the original Hanford's. We'll be attending the grand reopening."

"What will we actually be doing?"

He slid his water glass from side to side, spreading the puddle of condensation across the wood tabletop. "It's just your standard grin and grip."

At her questioning look, he clarified, "That means we smile for the camera while shaking the hands of local dignitaries. Along the same lines as baby kissing."

Rachel didn't want to think about kissing at all. "So how long will that grinning and gripping take?"

"An hour — two, tops." Then his expression turned gloom. "But I have a feeling my father might have scheduled some surprises for us, so it could take longer."

"The last time your father surprised us, we ended up 'married.'"

Jack gave her a sour look. "Maybe he's scheduled a quickie 'divorce.'"

"That would be great, wouldn't it?" she said with a high laugh that sounded false even to her own ears.

"Wonderful," he agreed, digging in his

pocket and tossing out a few bills for a tip. "Why don't you head up to the room while I pay the check?"

Rachel pushed back her chair and rose. "Thanks," she said brightly. "I am pretty tired."

She strode past him out of the restaurant, then cut across the hotel lobby toward the elevators. She hugged her purse close to her as she rode up to their floor, trying to ignore the ache digging away at her. But as much as she might try to deny it, it had hurt to hear Jack's eagerness at terminating their pretense of a marriage.

She let herself into their suite and headed straight for her bedroom. She made sure the door was locked behind her before she stripped off her clothes and threw her knee-length nightgown over her head. Knowing she'd never fall asleep so early after her nap in the car, she turned on the television and flipped through the endless cable channels.

She'd just settled on an old black-and-white screwball comedy when Jack knocked on her door. "Rachel?" he called out.

She hit the mute button, glad the door was still locked. "Yes?"

"Do you need anything?" he asked. "Is there anything I can get for you?"

Yes, she thought, *you.* "I'm fine, thanks."

She sensed him hesitating outside the door, imagined him raking his thick, brown hair with his fingers. "Okay, then," he called out finally, "I'll see you in the morning."

When she heard his footsteps retreating to his side of the suite, she turned the sound back on and settled back to enjoy the movie. But although she'd always laughed the twenty other times she'd seen the old film, nothing they did seemed funny any more.

She zapped the TV off with the remote and pulled out her book again. An hour later, after rereading the same page three times, she gave up on the murder mystery and flipped off the light.

Despite the dark, despite the quiet, it took a long time for sleep to claim her.

The late-morning April sun slanted across the parking lot of the Hanford House of Pancakes in Clintonville, burning the chrome of the cars into an eye-hurting dazzle. Squinting against the brightness, Jack gazed out at the milling crowd as his and Rachel's first restaurant appearance sputtered to a close.

He wiggled his shoulders, trying to release a knot of tension, the progeny of too little sleep and too much stress. The stress had its usual source — the breathless waiting for the other shoe to drop, for the usual culmination into calamity of one of his father's schemes. The photographs had been taken, the crowd was about to disperse, but Jack wasn't uncrossing his fingers just yet.

The lack of sleep had a more delectable cause — and she was standing next to him right now in front of the restaurant. Far too close to give him any hope of relaxing the tightness in his shoulders, Rachel teased him like his brief, scattered dreams from last night. A vision in a trim shirtdress of turquoise and black, jet earrings winking at him from her ears, she strained his self-control and kicked aside his good intentions.

He dragged in a long breath, then wished he hadn't. He'd expected her to wear some kind of floral scent, something light and innocent. Instead, her fragrance tangled his thoughts and jangled his nerves with a hint of spice, a touch of musk. The subtle, delicious scent invited him to taste her.

Setting his jaw, Jack forced his thoughts away from Rachel. The interning reporter and camerawoman from the local television station, having finished the uneventful interview, chatted quietly off to one side. The photographer from Hanford's publicity department squeezed off a last few shots of the remodeled restaurant's exterior, recording the event for posterity and the next annual report. Ralph, the restaurant manager, beaming at the attention given his newly refurbished location, spoke animatedly with the stringer from the local newspaper.

The introduction of "Mr. and Mrs. Hanford" had come off smoothly. Was it possible they'd sidestepped the usual disaster?

"It went well, didn't it?" Rachel asked, smiling up at him.

The curve of her mouth distracted him a moment before he answered, "So far, so good."

Her smile dimmed a bit. "Did I do okay?"

He saw the insecurity in her face and realized she might have misinterpreted his edginess as a reflection on her. "You," he said, allowing himself to run a playful finger along her soft cheek, "performed admirably. Despite all the fuss, despite those hideous stand-ups." He gestured at the cardboard cut-outs of the two of them leering from the doorway, a sign proclaiming them "Mr. and Mrs. Hanford" propped at their cardboard feet.

She grimaced at the life-sized facsimiles. "I don't suppose we could burn those?"

"Knowing my father, he's got a hundred backups."

She groaned. "A hundred 'Rachels' out

there with the same goofy look on their faces."

"Yours looks fine," he told her. "Mine's the one that resembles an ax murderer. All it needs is a hockey mask."

"They both look like something out of a horror film," she said. *"Welcome to the Hanford House of Pancakes,"* she intoned, *"your first stop into the* Twilight Zone."

"We could sneak back after hours," he suggested. "Squirrel them away in the trunk of the car."

She laughed. "We'd have enough for a bonfire by the end of the trip."

Inexplicably, her final words, "end of the trip" set off a hollow ache inside him. Ridiculous, he told himself. He really wanted nothing more than to have the tour finished and behind him.

He pushed aside the incomprehensible feeling and smiled at her. "I think we're done here. Let's say our good-byes to the manager and head back to the hotel."

She nodded and followed him over to where the manager held court. The man pumped Jack's hand enthusiastically, then gave Rachel's fingers a squeeze.

"This has been great, Mr. Hanford," the manager said. "What a jump-start for the business."

Maybe his father's scheme wasn't so hare-brained if it made the franchise managers happy. The tension tickling the back of Jack's neck released a fraction. "We're glad to help."

Ralph gestured toward the restaurant. "Once we get the photos of you two in the costume, you guys can get out of here."

The tenseness resumed its grip. "Costume?"

"The Mr. Pancake costume," Ralph clarified. "It's in the storeroom. You can change there."

An urgency to leave filled Jack as the manager escorted them inside the restaurant. He shot a quick look of desperation at Rachel. She shrugged, shaking her head.

The manager rambled on. "I had my doubts about it, but your dad seemed to think it would be the highlight of the grand reopening."

"What's he talking about?" Rachel whispered as they passed through the kitchen.

"I don't know," Jack told her. "But I have a very bad feeling about this."

Ralph led them to the storeroom and flipped on the light. There, amongst the packed shelves laden with industrial-sized cans of syrup and massive bags of Hanford's pancake mix, was a curious pile of brown material.

"You just step into it here," the manager said, "then after you have Mrs. Hanford on your shoulders —"

"On my shoulders?" Jack cut in.

"— I'll help you pull the costume up the rest of the way," the man finished.

Jack just stared down at the mass of brown fabric and padding, an all-too-clear image in his mind of Rachel balanced on his shoulders, her legs wrapped around his neck. His gaze flicked to her modest shirt-dress, and his imagination added the sensation of her heat warming him through her sheer hose.

Rachel's wide-eyed gaze fixed on the costume. "Why do I have to get on Jack's shoulders?"

"It's a two-person costume," Ralph told her. "You have to work the arms."

Jack gritted his teeth so hard, he thought his jaw would permanently lock. "I'm going to kill my father," he muttered.

"I'll help you," Rachel concurred.

As if a snake waited for him in the costume's folds, Jack stepped cautiously inside it. He crouched down and shot Rachel a challenging look. Her lower lip caught in her teeth, she moved behind him.

"Could you get a little lower, please?" she asked.

He bent his shoulders down a bit more. She hooked one shapely leg over his shoulder, then the other. She teetered a moment, and he had to steady her, his hands spanning her thighs, her warmth teasing his palms.

"Ready?" he rasped out.

"Yes," she answered softly.

He rose, her light weight little burden to the strong muscles of his thighs. Ralph followed him up with the costume.

"This is how you work the arms," Ralph said to Rachel. He demonstrated, and Jack could see them flap on either side of him.

Then Rachel shifted as she pulled the top part of the costume on the rest of the way and closed it over their heads. Jack couldn't keep his mind from the juncture of her thighs resting against the back of his neck.

"We'll have to go out the back," Ralph said, his voice muted through the layers of costume.

Rachel squirmed again and Jack thought he would explode. "If you don't want me to drop you," he growled, "you'd better be still."

She froze, her legs locking around his

neck. "Sorry. Can you see? I can't see anything."

"I can see," Jack said as he followed Ralph from the restaurant and around the side to the front.

Ralph led them around to the entrance of the restaurant. "Work the arms," he said as he turned them to face the crowd. "Wave."

Jack could just see Mr. Pancake's hands flick in the periphery of his limited vision. Rachel's soft inner arms brushed against his hair with each movement. Her muscular calves melded themselves to his sides as she held her balance.

Jack wondered idly what evil he'd done in a former life to earn him this torture. "Ralph," he hissed. "How long do we have to be in the costume?"

"Just a few more pictures for the paper," the manager told him. "Then the kids."

Jack wasn't sure he wanted to know. "What about the kids?"

"The coloring contest winners," Ralph said. "They get one picture each."

Jack groaned, but he knew it was no use.

The photography session dragged on and on, while Jack distracted himself from the pair of womanly legs wrapped around his neck by devising creative ways to commit patricide. To counter the sweet agony of

100

Rachel's scent, Jack contemplated any number of appealing revenges against his father.

By the time they returned to the storeroom and Ralph peeled the costume off them again, Jack had contrived a hundred ingenious ways to send Henry Hanford to his deserved end. His body still a mass of nerve endings, Jack lowered Rachel back to earth, then gazed down at her.

Her flushed face, her mussed hair, the wrinkles in her dress, all reminded him of how she had been so intimately pressed against him. With a growl of frustration, Jack stomped out of the storeroom.

Death was much too good for Henry Hanford.

Chapter 5

Rachel glanced at Jack's stormy expression as he pulled the cherry-red rental car off I-64 and turned toward their hotel. "Are you angry?" she asked him.

"No," he snapped.

Rachel sighed and stared out the window. She thought about how her body had reacted to his touch on her legs, to the feel of him between her thighs. Could he tell? Was that why he was mad at her?

The red Camaro zoomed into the hotel parking lot, shuddering over a speed bump. "I just don't like being the victim of my father's harebrained schemes."

"I'm sorry," Rachel said softly.

Jack braked the car under the hotel canopy with a screech and turned to glare at her. "For what?"

She blinked at his fierce gaze. "I don't know. I just . . ."

Her voice trailed off as Jack's anger faded into tenderness. He reached out and drew a finger along her cheek. "You have nothing to apologize for, Rachel. This was Dad's doing."

Rachel suppressed a shiver at Jack's touch. "He does seem to enjoy messing with other people's lives."

Jack nodded thoughtfully, then his mouth slowly stretched into a grin. "I think vengeance is definitely in order."

Rachel smiled in response. "I agree. Between the two of us, we ought to come up with something suitable."

"Two days in the Mr. Pancake costume?" Jack suggested.

"Locked in a preschool full of three-year-olds," Rachel added.

"All on a sugar high from too many pancakes," Jack said.

A giggle tickled Rachel's throat. "What a picture."

"Can't you see the newspaper headlines?" Jack asked. *Hotcake Honcho Henry Hanford Harried by Hyperactive Hellions.*"

"Or *Mr. Pancake Eaten Alive by Hordes of Hoydens.*" Rachel could barely get the words out past her laughter.

Jack joined her, his deep voice a counterpoint to her lighter one. When their laughter had nearly abated, Jack pointed out the windshield at the parking valets watching them, open-mouthed, and that set them off again.

The laughter subsided again, leaving Rachel breathless and teary-eyed. She was surprised to realize her hand was linked with Jack's as if they'd both sought an anchor for the hilarity they'd shared. She shifted her fingers and her palm brushed against his.

Shyly, she raised her eyes to his. A trace of humor still lit his gaze, gently curved his mouth. But something else burned in the blue of his eyes, an emotion that burst past her frail good sense and straight into her heart.

His gaze flicked down to her mouth. Sensation shivered up her spine as she imagined him grazing his lips across hers, tasting her. Then he tugged at her hand, and pulled her closer.

Their first kiss was a whisper of contact. She might have thought that only his breath had brushed against her lips, his heat had pressed against her. Then his free hand curved up around the back of her neck and her musing thoughts exploded.

His mouth covered hers, slanting against her soft lips, sipping at the sensitive skin. The first touch of his tongue left her gasping, had her parting her lips to give him access. His tongue swept inside her mouth in a brief foray, then thrust in again for another taste.

A moan escaped her lips, the sound trembling along her flesh, heightening every sensation. Somehow, her hands had moved to his chest, diving inside his suit jacket to skim across his chest. The smooth fabric of his shirt warmed under her palms, tempting her to slip her fingers beneath to feel his firm male skin.

Jack's large hand curved at her waist, urging her toward him. She wanted to crawl into his lap, crawl inside him, nestle in his heart. Shyly at first, then more boldly, she plunged her tongue into his mouth, giddy with the heady feeling. She could stay here forever, kissing him, touching him and being touched by him.

A tapping sounded dimly in Rachel's brain. She ignored it, angling her mouth to fit more snugly against Jack's. The tapping grew louder, accompanied by an imploring voice. She dimly registered the muffled words, "We have to move your car, Mr. Hanford," but ignored them as trivial.

It wasn't until Jack pulled back and set her away from him that Rachel realized she'd been making quite a spectacle of herself in front of a very appreciative audience. Heat rising in her cheeks, she looked around her at the circle of grinning parking valets.

"Oh, my heavens," she moaned, hands covering her face. "What am I doing?"

"What are *we* doing?" Jack muttered.

She shot him a quick glance. As she watched, he brought one hand up to rake his hair back and she could swear his fingers shook. Then he clutched the steering wheel as if he'd like to wrench it from the car. Could he be as affected by their kiss as she?

"Let's get inside," he said, his tone neutral, as if nothing unusual had just passed between them.

Rachel tried to ignore the sharp disappointment that lanced through her. What did she expect? He'd probably kissed dozens of women, all of them no doubt more beautiful than her. He might have garnered some enjoyment from their kiss, but it surely wasn't any big deal to him.

He swung out of the car in one lithe movement and tossed the keys to the head valet. She was grateful when he came around to open her door and help her from the car; she wasn't sure she could have gained her feet on her own. It didn't really matter that he let go of her hand as soon as she was standing.

She stepped into the revolving door ahead of him, fingers digging into the purse at her side. She waited for him to come through, then they walked side by side to the elevators.

"Are you hungry?" he asked as they stepped into the elevator car.

She checked her watch and was surprised to see it was past noon. She supposed she should be hungry, but the pancakes they'd eaten at the restaurant early this morning still sat like a lump in her stomach.

"Not really," she told him, fixing her gaze on the cleft in his chin, afraid to meet his eyes.

The doors slid open on their floor. "Rachel."

She slipped out of the elevator car and headed down the hall toward their suite. "Rachel," he called again as she reached the door and fumbled for the key card.

"Hey," he said, catching up with her. When she refused to look up at him, his warm hand captured her chin and turned her toward him. "I'm sorry," he said softly.

That was the worst thing he could have said, that he was sorry he'd kissed her. Despite her best intentions, tears caught at her throat, gathered in her eyes. "You don't need to apologize," she said, the words scraping from her throat.

"I do," he said, lifting her chin higher. "I was out of line — again."

She forced herself to smile. "It was nothing, really." Then she tossed her head away from his warm hand and jammed the key card into the lock. When the green light glowed, she shoved the door open in relief and headed straight for her room.

"Rachel!"

She stopped with her hand on the knob, then turned slowly to face him. "Yes?"

He ran his fingers through his hair, then thrust his hands into his pants pockets. He shifted from one foot to the other, looked at the floor, examined the ceiling, then finally raised his eyes to hers.

"Do you want to go skating?"

She shook her head, thinking she hadn't heard him right. "What?"

"Go skating," he repeated. "We passed a rink on the way back to the hotel."

Rachel hesitated, suspicious of his invitation. "I don't know how," she said.

"You've never been on skates?" he asked.

"I have," she told him, "But my feet don't cooperate, and my arms flap around and the next thing you know I'm flat on my behind."

"I can help you learn," he said, his irresistible grin melting her heart.

She couldn't help but smile in return. "I doubt I can make it around the rink even once without falling."

"Then I'll hold you up." Jack took a hesitant step toward her. "What do you say? We don't have anything else scheduled until tomorrow morning."

The tightness in her middle dispersed. "I'd love to. Just let me change into jeans."

"Me, too." He moved toward his bedroom. "Meet you out here in ten minutes."

She nodded agreement and pushed open her door. Toeing off her shoes, she headed for the closet holding her hanging bag, and tugged out a T-shirt and jeans. As she changed, she couldn't suppress the smile that kept returning to her face.

Be careful, a little inner voice called to her. *Don't let yourself be too happy. Remember, it will all be over very soon.*

"But I might as well enjoy it now," she told her reflection as she dashed a comb through her hair. Then, her step light, she hurried back out to Jack.

A half-hour later, seated on one of the benches placed along the periphery of the roller rink, loud rock music battering her ears, Rachel entertained a host of second thoughts. "Maybe I should just stay here," she said, tapping together the roller skates laced onto her feet.

"No way," Jack said, the in-line skates he'd chosen adding inches to his already impressive height. "There's not much of a crowd. You'll be fine."

"I'm very comfortable here," she said, patting the bench beneath her. She gestured at the walls of the indoor rink, decorated with colorful murals of Illinois history. "I can look at the paintings."

"You'll get a better view skating." He balanced easily on his skates, one hand lightly touching the outer rail of the rink. "Just hold on to me."

Rachel teetered to her feet. "We'll fall on our backsides together, no doubt." She clutched the rail, groping out with her free hand for Jack. "Lead on."

One hand linked in hers, the other on the rail, he guided her down the two steps leading into the rink. They moved out of the way of the stairs, then waited, holding on, while a pair of seniors sailed by arm-in-arm. The gray-haired woman waved as she passed, tossing off a cheerful smile.

Rachel watched as the elderly couple turned in tandem to glide backward around the far curve of the rink. "This is when you're supposed to say, 'if they can do it — ' "

110

"— we can do it," he finished for her. "Never mind those two. They've probably been skating together for decades."

Just as Rachel thought she might be ready to let go, another pair zoomed by, their four-year-old legs pumping madly. The mother of the twin girls followed in their wake, calling out warnings to slow down and watch out for other skaters.

Rachel laughed as the little girls elbowed each other for skating room. "Maybe we should just go back to the hotel."

"Not a chance," Jack said, tugging at her arm. "We can't let a pair of preschoolers show us up."

They shoved away from the railing, Rachel's legs wobbling under her. She hung on to Jack for dear life, one arm snaked around his waist, the other plastered against his where it rested just above her hip. Their forward motion creaked to a stop.

"I suppose we have to move now," she said, staring down at her skate-encased toes.

"That would make it more like actual skating," Jack said. He peered down at her, a smile teasing the corner of his mouth. "Ready?"

She nodded, and on the count of three, they pushed off. Rachel's knees still trembled, but with Jack's body supporting hers, she felt her confidence growing.

"It's a miracle," she said breathlessly. "I'm still on my feet."

"Teamwork," Jack said, snugging her more tightly against him.

They moved with a rhythm, swaying together as they crept slowly around the rink. Now that she wasn't so terrified of having her feet fly out from under her, Rachel became more aware of the man beside her. Specifically, how his body felt pressed against hers from shoulder to hip.

Without conscious thought, her fingers curved more tightly against the soft blue knit of his T-shirt, the heat of him soaking into her palm. The muscles in his back flexed in response, rippling against her arm.

The fingers of her other hand had linked with his, holding him against the first swell of her hip. She could feel his touch through the thickness of the heavy denim she wore. She could imagine all too well his fingers dipping inside the waist of her jeans, stroking the sensitive skin there.

Rachel redirected her attention to the vivid mural on the wall as they rolled past, of French explorers Joliet and Marquette. "I never learned much Illinois history," she said.

"Native Hoosier?" he asked as he increased their speed slightly.

"Born and raised." She matched her pace to his, enjoying the feel of their bodies moving together. "How about you?"

"Born in Chicago, although we've lived all over the state." Jack pulled her closer. "Watch out!"

The twin terrors on skates dove around them, one of the little girls banging against Rachel's leg. Rachel teetered and would have fallen if Jack hadn't held on tight, his balance aided by the railing.

Her heart beat in a rapid tattoo, a consequence of the near miss and Jack's arm around her, holding her to his chest. Rachel's palms were spread against the hard muscles and she was loath to move away. But she forced herself to push back and use the rail for support instead of Jack.

"Are you okay?" he asked, his blue eyes fixed on hers.

"Fine," she said, looking away. A mural of Abraham Lincoln stared down at her, his eyes mournful. "In fact, I think I'm finally getting the hang of this. I'd like to try it on my own."

He smiled down at her. "Let's not rush things." He held out his hand.

Rachel hesitated, then laid her palm

against his. He moved off with her beside him, linked only by their hands. But if Rachel thought less contact would be easier to handle, she was sorely mistaken.

A heated energy seemed to jolt up her arm each time she swung it in concert with his. She might not be in contact with his long legs, the muscles in his torso, but the rhythm of his movement translated into his arm and hand so that she was acutely aware of each motion of his body.

And although she felt steadier on her feet, her increasing freedom of movement as she glided along only heightened her awareness of Jack. She almost felt as if she were flying as they skated faster and faster around the rink, the wash of color on the walls becoming a blur. When they passed the racing preschoolers, Rachel threw back her head and laughed, the joy of motion and color whirling inside her.

Suddenly Jack turned and caught her other hand, skating backwards as he faced her. "What are you doing?" she gasped.

He grinned, a wild look in his eyes. "I'm either being very daring or very stupid."

Rachel's hands tightened reflexively on his. "How can you see where you're going?"

"I can't," he said, his grin widening. "I'm counting on you for that."

She couldn't help the little shriek that escaped her as they neared a more slowly skating pair. "Behind you!" she warned, tugging his left arm to guide him to safety.

They passed the couple with room to spare, but Rachel's arms trembled from the effort. "Here comes the corner," she told him, urging him to take the turn.

They whipped around the corner without mishap, then settled into the straightaway. Jack laughed, the sound shuddering through Rachel as they picked up speed again. Rachel forgot their surroundings, the other skaters, the music blaring from unseen speakers. All her being focused on Jack, on the feel of his hands locked with hers, the motion of his body as he urged her along, the tension of their connection and his faith in her guidance of him.

His face was fierce with excitement, and she shared that emotion as their entire world narrowed down to each other. When they reached the next corner, she didn't speak, wasn't aware of even shifting her weight or tightening her fingers, but he somehow caught her signal, making the turn in a strong, fluid curve. She felt she could close her eyes and still guide him, her thoughts linked with his, their minds and bodies in tandem.

He broke the spell then, slowing as they reached the next turn, his strong arms pulling her around to a dizzying stop. He didn't release her, just tugged her more tightly into the corner out of the way of the passing skaters. His chest heaved with the effort of their skating and his face still shone with the same wildness.

"I have to kiss you again," he said, his even voice just audible above the blast of music.

She shook her head. "Jack, please," she whispered.

"Please, don't?" he asked, lowering his head to her. "Or please, do?"

She was unable to answer when he was so close. A million words scrambled through her brain, but none of them had the courtesy of stringing together in a sensible fashion. It was like dropping a string of beads and watching them scatter.

She made a sound, to discourage him, but invited him instead. She tipped her head, to dissuade him, but the motion only encouraged him. She knew because her logical brain wasn't directing her anymore, only her instincts, which said she wanted very badly to kiss Jack again.

"Ah, Rachel," he murmured, then closed the distance between them.

If she expected an all-out embrace like the

one in the car, she was at once disappointed and relieved. Disappointed because every fiber of her being was ready for that kind of kiss, relieved because they were, after all, in a public place and on display. So when he only sipped at her lips, only teased with the tip of his tongue without venturing inside, she relaxed into his caresses. She even tilted her head to give him easier access.

Jack kept his hands on her shoulders, his thumbs moving lazily across the knit of her T-shirt. She could feel his arms tremble as if he wanted to pull her closer, but didn't dare. His control made her feel safe, made the feelings welling inside her less frightening.

Then he pulled back from her, and his gaze burned into hers. His hands flexed in a hypnotic massage.

"Had enough skating?" he asked softly, his intent look sending shivers through her.

She swallowed against the alarming sensation. "Yes. I'd like to go back."

He cocked a smile at her, then leaned in to nip brief kisses on her lips, her cheek. "Your room?" he asked, his lips brushing her ear, "or mine?"

At first Rachel didn't understand, then the sense of what he'd said seeped in. She stumbled back from him, then had to grope for the rail when she teetered. Her fingers clutching the wooden dowel, she shook her head, sending her hair flying.

"N-neither," she stuttered, eyes wide. "I mean, both. I mean —"

Her tumble of words cut off at his broad grin as he glided closer to her. She felt like an utter fool as he leaned against the rail, keeping a foot of space between them.

"You were joking," she realized, praying he couldn't hear the trace of disappointment in her tone.

"I'm sorry," he said. "I've embarrassed you."

She thrust her chin up at him, mustering as much dignity as she could on her wobbly skates. "Not at all," she lied. "But you said you wouldn't touch me anymore. You can understand how I could misconstrue the joke."

His mouth curved in a wry smile. "I did promise to behave myself. Unfortunately, you keep testing my resistance."

Rachel gave him a cross look, although she knew very well she'd been a wholeheartedly willing participant. "We can't keep doing this. It isn't right," she said primly.

"That's the problem," he said softly. "It's far too right."

What in heaven's name did that mean? Afraid to delve too deeply into what he'd said, Rachel pushed off from the rail, struggling for a moment to maintain her balance without Jack's weight beside her. She cut across the rink, avoiding the fast-moving skaters as she headed for the exit.

He caught up with her as she reached the steps, his hand on her elbow helping her up them. She eased herself onto a bench with a sigh, tensing again immediately when he sat beside her.

She got an excellent view of his broad back when he leaned down to unlace his skates. He looked up at her over his shoulder, catching her drooling.

"Hungry?" he asked.

Very. Aloud, she said, "Getting there."

"Want to go out again?" he asked, giving her skate lace a playful tug. "Or order in?"

She loosened the laces, then toed off her skates in relief. "How early do we leave tomorrow?"

"We have to be at the BigMart in Hedley by nine. That's an hour's drive from here."

"So, up by seven." She rubbed at her tired eyes. "Dinner in, I think."

She didn't want to consider how tempting it would be to share a meal in the intimacy of the suite. She was a grown-up, she could keep her emotions under control.

Grabbing her sneakers from the cubby

where she'd left them, she tugged them on, then bent to scoop up the skates. Before she could rise on her own, Jack reached down to help her to her feet and the grin he gave her nearly stopped her heart.

"Thank you," she murmured, juggling the skates as an excuse to pull her hand from his. She followed him to the skate return, looking forward to the coming evening with a disconcerting mix of anticipation and dread.

Jack was still kicking himself over his "your place or mine" crack even after the bellman had cleared away the last of the room service dishes. It had earned him Rachel's constant wariness during dinner, her polite distancing throughout the meal. She probably didn't even enjoy the butter-tender filet, she was so on edge waiting for him to make another pass.

And now she sat on the sofa opposite him, her feet tucked under her, her back ramrod straight as she read her book. At least, she pretended to read; he hadn't seen her turn a page for the last several minutes. His presence probably set her on edge. If he was any kind of a gentleman, he'd take his laptop computer into his bedroom and catch up on his work there.

Rachel must have sensed his eyes on her

because she looked up at him. "What?" she asked.

"Nothing." His fingers fidgeted on the keyboard as he cast about for something to say. "Good book?"

She turned the book to look at the cover, making a face. "It was at first. The middle's kind of slow." She gestured with the paperback. "What are you doing?"

"Spreadsheets," he said, then laughed at her expression. "Real exciting stuff."

She smiled. "Maybe more riveting than this book." She tossed the novel aside. "Do you like old movies?"

He blinked at the sudden change in subject. "Some."

"*The African Queen* comes on in five minutes, I can go watch it in the other room, or —"

"Go ahead and turn it on," he said, powering down the laptop and setting it aside. "I could use a break."

Rachel rose and switched on the massive television positioned between the two sofas. "It's a favorite of mine," she said, then hesitated, her gaze moving from his sofa to the one opposite.

Jack patted the seat next to him. "I won't bite." At her frankly dubious look, he added, "I promise."

Her slow smile had his heart stuttering and he wondered if having her next to him was such a great idea after all. Then she scooted onto the sofa and curled up beside him.

When he curved an arm around her, she stiffened for a moment, then relaxed, and nestled against him. As the credits for *The African Queen* rolled across the television screen, Jack resisted the urge to pull Rachel even closer to his side. His senses filled with her scent and the feel of her silky hair against his cheek, he settled back to enjoy the movie.

Her dreams were filled with a tumble of images of Charlie Allnutt and Rose Sayer, the Congo and the *African Queen*. Except, Jack's face would seep in to take the place of Humphrey Bogart's and her own seemed superimposed over that of Katharine Hepburn. She woke with a sense that she'd slept the night in Jack's arms, although they'd parted when the movie's final credits rolled on the television screen.

The continental breakfast provided by the hotel was a quiet affair. Rachel sipped juice and nibbled on fussy, too-sweet pastries as she gazed appreciatively across the table at Jack in his trim, gray suit and Hanford's corporate tie. She'd worn the coral skirt and blouse, blushing when he complimented her on how lovely she looked in it.

The hour's drive to Hedley passed with few words between them, as well. It wasn't so much that Rachel had nothing to say, but she still basked in the glow of their companionable night together. That was where she wanted to leave their relationship — a comfortable friendship without all the intense intimacy of the skating trip yesterday.

But when they pulled into the BigMart parking lot and Rachel looked over at Jack, she realized that she'd only been fooling herself. His eyes locked with hers, the lake blue darkening imperceptibly as if clouded by a brief storm of passion. And darn her traitorous heart, she wanted to dive right in.

She tore her gaze away from his, trembling as he pulled the Camaro into a parking slot. But the sizzling energy the quick exchange had sparked through her had settled into her very being, speeded her heart rate, her breathing. She dragged air into her lungs, feeling like a runner who thought she'd finished a race and discovered she had another two laps to go.

The cordiality of the night before dispersed, replaced by something more dangerous. She supposed it was her own fault; after all those years of fantasizing, the real thing was all the more potent. What she had to remember was that as real as Jack might be, he was also temporary, and a husband in name only.

She turned to him with a bright smile. "Ready?"

He stared out the windshield a moment before facing her. "I enjoyed watching the movie with you last night."

"Me, too," she said, gathering up her purse and placing it in her lap like a barrier. "*The African Queen*'s one of my favorites."

"It wasn't the movie," he said, tucking a strand of her hair behind her ear. "It was being with you."

Her heart did a little dance in her chest. "I liked being with you, too," she ventured.

His finger lingered on her cheek. "I've been thinking —"

A sharp rap on the driver-side window cut off whatever Jack had been about to say. Rachel glared at the interloper, annoyed that some of the best moments in her life were being interrupted by people banging on the car window.

Jack's friendly smile at the woman on the other side of the glass only enhanced Rachel's irritation. "Loretta!" he called out as he pushed open the car door.

Rachel eased from her side of the car and watched sourly as Jack pulled the dark-haired Loretta into his arms for a far too familiar hug. It took all the self-control Rachel could muster to keep from slamming the car door as Jack's clinch with the brunette goddess went on far too long for even a pretend wife's peace of mind.

Chin high, purse clutched to her side like a shield, Rachel marched around the Camaro. Jack and the brunette had put some space between them, but their arms were still linked as they faced each other. Loretta was gazing adoringly up at Jack and Rachel could have sworn Jack's soft smile answered that admiration.

She thrust her hand out between the two. "Rachel Reeves," she said, waiting for Loretta to let go of Jack.

The woman did, her gray eyes flicking over Rachel as she gripped her proffered hand. "Loretta Hanford. You must be the little wife." She laughed. "Henry certainly comes up with some crazy schemes."

Rachel took a hopeful breath. "Jack's sister?"

"Distant cousin, actually." She beamed a smile at Jack. "From the Springfield branch of the family."

Loretta's gaze swept Rachel, then dismissed her as she seemed to realize Rachel presented no threat. She leaned toward Jack, linked her arm with his. "We're kissing cousins, really."

If Rachel had hoped for a denial from Jack, she was disappointed. He just laughed, accepting the buss Loretta gave him on his cheek as if it were one of many they'd shared. Loretta's smug look said more than words that the woman had some kind of prior claim on Jack.

Jack offered Rachel the crumb of his other arm and the three of them started for the BigMart entrance. "What brings you down here, Loretta?"

She flashed a flawless smile up at him. "Your father, actually. He wanted me here to make sure things went smoothly." Loretta tossed Rachel a glance, as if she suspected any potential problems would be Rachel's doing.

"Any idea what he's planning today?" Jack asked.

"He didn't say, exactly," Loretta answered. "Just a celebration of the mutual BigMart-Hanford's promotion, I assume."

As they reached the front of the massive warehouse store, the manager of the store flagged down Loretta. "Excuse me," she said as she headed off to speak to him.

Rachel could feel the tension in Jack's arm as they stood gazing out over the parking lot. "I hope he isn't expecting Mr. Pancake to make another appearance."

Rachel looked up at him. "Is he likely to do the same nutty thing twice?"

Jack made a wary scan of the crowd. "He's really more like lightning. I would bet Hanford's last bottle of syrup he's got something new up his sleeve."

Someone jostled them from behind and Rachel looked down to find a towheaded six-year-old boy gazing up at her with an engaging grin. She smiled at him, then returned her attention to her survey of the parking lot.

"What's that noise?" Jack asked, looking skyward.

A buzzing dug at Rachel's ears and grew in volume. She placed a hand on Jack's shoulder. "It's a small plane. What does that sign say that it's towing?"

Jack squinted into the morning brightness.

"*The sky's the limit at Hanford House of Pancakes,*" he read from the fluttering message.

The plane roared by, dragging the sign, then made a wide turn. *Come Try the Hanford-BigMart Special,* the other side read.

Loretta returned and graced Jack with her perfect smile. "That's great! That'll bring in the crowds."

But Jack was still on edge, and Rachel had had enough of a taste of Henry Hanford's style to know they weren't in the clear yet. As they watched the plane make another turn, she and Jack shared a worried glance.

"Bobby! Bobby, you stop that!" a woman's voice called out behind them. "What are you doing?"

Rachel felt the little boy brush against them again, but she was too distracted by the plane to notice what he was doing. Then she felt the chill of steel around her wrist, and a tug. She pulled her arm away in reaction, then stared agog at the handcuff that linked her to Jack.

"Bobby," the boy's mother cried out, "you give me the key, right now."

"Don't have no keys," the towhead told her. "The man didn't give 'em to me."

"What man?" his mother asked him.

The little boy stuck his lower lip out. "The man that told me to put 'em on the man and the lady."

Jack shot a quick glance at Rachel, then he went down on one knee, his arm suspended by the handcuff. "Bobby," he said to the little boy. "What did this man look like?"

Bobby shrugged. "He was old. He said I could have the handcuffs when you were through with them. Can I have 'em now?"

Jack rose, lifting the cuffs to have a closer look. "Toy handcuffs usually have a release button." He turned their wrists over. "These don't. I think they're real."

"Henry Hanford has struck again," Rachel said, raising her voice over the roar of the plane that was nearly overhead again.

"Maybe the local police could help us with these," Jack shouted.

"What's that?" Loretta called out, distracting them from the problem of the handcuffs. "Look! There must be hundreds of them, falling from the plane."

Rachel stared in disbelief. "Oh, my."

"Pancakes," Jack murmured, his tone a mix of awe and dread.

And as they watched, the rain of flapjacks fluttered and wheeled, like doughy birds against the bright blue sky. Then the first one hit the pavement and the riot ensued.

Chapter 6

As she stooped to snatch up another pancake fragment, Rachel struggled to wipe the grin from her face. But despite her efforts, she couldn't quite squelch the pleasant memory of that four-inch flapjack dropping squarely on Loretta's expertly coiffed head. Allowing herself an unrepentant chuckle, she recalled Loretta's indignant screech, the way she pawed at her head to remove the offending mess.

"What's so funny?" Jack asked, as he bent with her to scoop up a pancake. He tossed it into the plastic trash bag they held together with their handcuffed hands.

"Nothing," Rachel said, unable to suppress a giggle.

Rachel dropped the bit of flapjack into the trash bag, then bent with Jack for the next one. She *was* sorry Loretta had nearly gotten trampled by the horde of children scrambling for pancakes. The brunette had been so busy picking gluey dough from her hair she'd been oblivious to the stampeding schoolchildren. Rachel couldn't quite suppress the satisfaction she felt that Jack had pulled her to safety when the children had swarmed, leaving Loretta to fend for herself.

"What are we going to do with that man?" Jack asked as he peeled a pancake from the hood of a mini-van.

"What we ought to do," Rachel said, scraping the last of a pancake from her hand, "is ship the whole mess to him."

"Serve Dad right to have a bundle of gooey pancakes dumped on his desk." He took the trash bag from her, setting it down on the pavement. "I hope Loretta found someone to help us out with these cuffs."

Rachel stepped closer to him to ease the tension on her wrist. "It's not so bad. It certainly encourages cooperation."

He smiled down at her, his knuckles grazing against hers. "Yes, it does," he said softly. "Keeps you right where I want you, too."

Rachel thought she might melt into the pavement like a pat of butter. Jack's head tipped down toward her, his lips parted slightly.

"I found a locksmith!" Loretta called out, and Jack's head jerked as if his cousin s voice had pulled him out of a daze.

Rachel watched Loretta approach with a heavyset man on her heels. The man set down a large metal toolbox and rummaged through it.

"Got just the thing," the locksmith said, pulling out a long, slender tool. A few flicks of the wrist and Rachel felt the handcuff release.

She pulled her hand to her and rubbed at her wrist. The locksmith opened Jack's side and they were both freed.

"I'll bet that's a relief," Loretta said.

Jack took Rachel's hand and examined her wrist. "Are you okay?"

"Fine," she said, although she felt oddly bereft separated from him. "Are we done here?" she asked.

He looked around them at the parking lot, "I think so. We ought to hit the road. Get checked in at the next hotel."

Loretta curled her fingers around Jack's arm. "The store manager wanted to speak with you about something." She nodded imperiously at Rachel. "You'll take care of the trash, won't you?"

"I'll get it," Jack said, grabbing the bag. Digging out the keys to the Camaro, he handed them to Rachel. "Meet you at the car."

She watched Jack, Loretta and the lock-smith head for the store, Loretta clinging to Jack like syrup to a pancake. After Jack dumped the trash in a bin, he and Loretta disappeared inside.

Rachel burned to know what Jack's relationship with this so-called distant cousin was. Had they had an affair? An engagement? Kissing cousins, Loretta had said. Would he kiss her now, as he said his good-byes?

Rachel ground her teeth as she stalked off to the Camaro. Images of Loretta in Jack's arms hounded her as she wrenched open the car door and climbed inside. It was none of her business what Jack did with Loretta and she was a fool to get herself worked up about it.

But by the time Jack arrived at the Camaro and slid into the driver's seat, Rachel wanted to punch him. To cover her violent impulses, she began digging through her purse for her hairbrush, then nearly threw the whole bag out the window when she couldn't find it immediately. When she finally wrapped her hand around the plastic handle, she yanked the brush through her hair with such force, it brought tears to her eyes.

Oblivious to her agitation, Jack eased the

Camaro from its space and drove out of the lot onto the street. "We'll stay in Mount Vernon a few days," he said. "We're taping the television spot there at a Hanford's restaurant."

The mention of television distracted her momentarily from her stewing over Loretta. "You mean the commercials?"

He grimaced as he pulled onto I-64 and merged into traffic. "Mr. and Mrs. Hanford sharing a quiet breakfast — with a television crew looking on."

"Sounds like fun," she said, excited by the prospect of being on TV.

Jack gave her a dubious look. "The good news is I arranged the television spot, not my father. And to make sure everything's set at the restaurant, I've asked Loretta to come along."

Rachel's sour mood returned. "She's joining us on the tour?" She winced at how peevish she sounded, but she couldn't help herself.

If Jack sensed her dismay, he didn't react to it. "For now. She'll be following us to the hotel as soon as she wraps things up with BigMart."

A pall as dark as Loretta's hair settled on Rachel. "How nice for you to have her along," she said with forced sweetness.

"For me?" He glanced at her in surprise. "Yes, I suppose she'll be a help."

"I meant because she's such a . . . good friend." Rachel bit out the words.

He shrugged. "We played together as children."

As adults, too? Rachel wanted to ask, but she didn't dare. "What does she do for Hanford's?"

Jack flipped on the Camaro's blinker and turned onto the exit at the I-57 junction. "Loretta's our corporate attorney. Handles contracts, that sort of thing."

Rachel subsided into miserable silence. How could she compete with such a paragon? Loretta was beautiful and bright, with an important job — not something as meaningless as being a seamstress.

She had to know, had to ask. "Were you two ever . . . close?"

He turned the Camaro into the Ramada Inn parking lot and pulled up to the lobby. "We've always been friends," he said carefully, eyes out the windshield.

He swung out of the car and handed the keys to the valet before crossing around to her side. She should have left it at that, but it nagged at her. "I meant, more than friends," she said when he helped her out of the car.

He seemed exasperated by her persistence. "There was a time when we thought we might marry."

Her stomach clenched at the thought. "But you didn't."

He escorted her into the hotel and across the lobby. "At that time, neither of us was ready."

Implying that they might be ready now. Rachel didn't want to know any more.

"I've got to book a room for Loretta," Jack said. He peered down at her. "Are you okay?"

Rachel gave him an artificially sunny smile. "Fine. Just a little hungry since we skipped lunch."

He tapped her chin. "Then we'll get you something to eat as soon as we get settled."

As he strode toward the check-in, Rachel's insides churned. She wouldn't be able to eat a bite. She'd have to come up with a good excuse to explain why she'd suddenly lost her appetite.

An hour later, when Loretta Hanford presented her glamorous self at the door to Jack and Rachel's suite, Rachel didn't need an excuse. One glimpse of Jack's gorgeous cousin sidling up to him was enough to give her an immediate, very painful, and quite genuine headache.

***

Jack checked his watch for probably the hundredth time during the meal as Loretta took a last bite of her shrimp scampi. He glanced up at his cousin, catching yet another slow, seductive look on her face, one that once might have aroused him. Instead it just gave him heartburn.

He quickly returned his gaze to his plate and bulldozed the pile of fettuccine with his fork, trying to make believe he'd eaten some of it. But all he could think of was Rachel, tension from her headache furrowing her brow, lacing her eyes with pain.

He forced himself to take a bite as he watched Loretta lift her wineglass. His cousin had been an active and challenging playmate as a girl and had grown into a sexy, voluptuous woman. A distant enough relative to satisfy propriety, he'd once considered her a suitable candidate were he to marry.

But now Loretta's generous good looks suddenly seemed blowzy and overblown. Her subtle come-ons during dinner had become an irritation. All he wanted now was to finish this interminable meal and return to Rachel.

Jack gave up on his dinner, pushing his plate away from him. "About ready?" he asked, dabbing at his mouth with his napkin.

Loretta swirled the pale golden liquid in her glass. "I thought I'd have dessert. That apple pie looks good."

His heart sank. "We could get some to go."

"I wanted it a la mode."

Eyes on him, she took a mouthful of the Chablis, then lapped the last traces of it with her tongue. The teasing gesture left Jack cold.

Jack's gaze roamed the restaurant, searching out the waiter. "Maybe you ought to try the cheesecake instead."

She'd sipped the last of her wine, then set her glass down with a sigh. Gesturing peremptorily for the waiter, she fixed him with her savvy blue gaze. "You're in love with her, aren't you?"

"No!" leaped out of his mouth before he could stop it. Then he backpedaled. "In love with who?" he asked, although he knew.

Her full mouth folding in a Cheshire cat smile, she said, "I think you can figure that one out."

Jack scowled at her, dragging out his Gold Card to pay the check. It was a preposterous idea — him in love with Rachel. He scarcely knew the woman. Not to mention the fact that he had no intention of falling in love with anyone. He'd leave that nonsense to his father.

Twenty minutes later, after walking Loretta to her room, Jack let himself into his and Rachel's suite. Rachel had left a lamp burning in the suite's living area, and its glow illuminated her slightly ajar door. The pale light barely cut the darkness of her bedroom, but the path it cast across the floor tempted him to follow it into her room.

He really should check on her. Her headache had seemed quite severe, from the way she'd rubbed at her temples, how it had stolen her appetite. What if she'd been lying there in pain all this time, waiting for him to return, to bring her something to ease her discomfort?

Moving quietly, Jack opened Rachel's door and slipped inside. Light spilled in from the living area, picking out the silhouette of her slender form stretched out on the bed. She'd fallen asleep with her clothes on, the bright coral of her skirt barely visible in the dim light.

If she hadn't even undressed for bed, her headache must have been as bad as he'd suspected. Eyes adjusting to the dimness, he could make out the lines of her body lying across the covers. Her hair had fallen to conceal her face and before he realized he'd moved, Jack had crossed the room to sweep the silky stuff back behind her ear. Then somehow, his hand remained there, curved against her cheek, soaking in the warmth of her delicate flesh as a thirsty plant drinks in water.

Moving carefully, he seated himself on the edge of her bed. As if she sensed his weight there, she shifted slightly toward him, one hand coming up to curl its fingers around his wrist. She murmured something unintelligible, snuggling into his hand, a faint smile on her face.

He ached to lie down beside her, to pull her into his arms and hold her all night. The shock of it was, the urge to be close to her had little to do with sensuality and everything to do with comfort. And not just for her, but for him. Rachel could fill the empty places inside him, the ones he chose to ignore. She could wash them clean, heal and soothe them, just with the beat of her heart against his.

A longing gripped him, pain that worked itself soul-deep. All he had to do to relieve the ache was to let her inside him, to open himself to her. A simple step as uncomplicated as pressing his lips against her satiny cheek.

He'd bent halfway to her, could nearly feel the warmth of her against his face when Loretta's words came back.

You're in love with her, aren't you?

He stopped, his mouth inches from the shell of her ear, his breath roiling her hair. Like soldiers in a matrimonial war, the stream of his stepmothers marched through his mind, each one the avowed love of his father's life, each one departing through the revolving door of divorce court within months or a bare handful of years.

It meant nothing. Love meant nothing. It brought two bodies together, enhanced their enjoyment of one another for a while, then faded like the promising pink of a sunrise.

Jack sat upright again. His heart seemed to twist in his chest as he slipped his arm from Rachel's gentle grip. He stood, ignoring the hollow that opened inside him as he retraced his steps and left Rachel's room.

His hand shook as he opened the door to his own room. He couldn't seem to calm its trembling as he undressed, no more than he could ease the tightness squeezing the back of his throat. He clenched his jaw against the unaccustomed emotion as he lay in his bed in stony silence.

The darkness closed around him like a cloak. But no amount of resolution, no fierce shutting of the doors to his heart could ease the pain there. And it was the pain that followed him into his sleep and into his dreams.

She was there before Rachel had even risen from bed.

Rachel woke, stiff from having slept too long in one position, and heard Loretta's voice in the other room. The woman's sultry tones were punctuated by Jack's deep laugh as the two shared some private joke.

Rachel sat up and stared balefully down at herself. The coral silk of her skirt and blouse were a mass of wrinkles and she didn't doubt her face looked the same. Her hair hung untidily over her eyes and she imagined her gloomy expression would be sufficient to frighten small children.

When she'd taken the pain reliever last night and had lain down to relax the headache away, she'd only wanted to escape. Just the thought of spending the evening with Jack and his gorgeous cousin, the two of them side-by-side a constant reminder of how perfect a match they were, was enough to send Rachel into hiding.

She'd intended to rest a few minutes until the headache eased, then call for room service. She'd never expected to fall asleep, let alone sleep through the night fully clothed. Now she had to face Jack and Loretta with a sleep-fogged brain and a wrinkled face.

Rising, she tugged the hem of her blouse free of her skirt and started to pull it over her head. She dropped the shirt back around her waist when she noticed her bedroom door was half-open. She could swear she'd left it nearly closed last night.

Rachel swung it shut, latching it quietly. She'd just as soon Jack and his cousin not know she was up yet. Quickly tossing aside her clothes, she headed for the bathroom and into a hot shower. She sighed as the spray coursed over her body, the water driving the last of the cobwebs from her brain.

Clean and refreshed, she crossed to the closet and flipped through the hangers for something to wear. They'd be taping the commercial today and Jack had told her the production company would be providing the clothes for the shoot. Going for comfort, she pulled an amethyst and royal blue skort from the closet, and a short-sleeved purple sweater to match. A pair of low-heeled, strappy sandals completed the outfit.

Her hair dried and tucked back neatly with two combs, Rachel figured she was as presentable as she was likely to get. She pasted a big smile on her face and strode through her bedroom door.

Her determined pace halted when she saw only Loretta standing in the living area. The dark-haired woman greeted Rachel with a smile that held just a trace of challenge, a faintly superior look in her blue eyes.

"Ready for your fifteen minutes of fame?" Loretta asked.

Rachel wiped suddenly damp palms on the folds of her skirt. "The commercial, you mean? I suppose I'm as ready as I'll ever be."

"I'm sure you'll do fine," Loretta said, although her tone implied otherwise.

"Where's Jack?" Rachel asked as casually as she could.

"He went down to check on a fax he was expecting." Loretta's smile broadened. "Just as well. I wanted to speak with you — alone."

Unease pooled in Rachel's stomach. "What about?"

"Jack, and me." Loretta leaned close. "I hope my relationship with him hasn't made you feel uncomfortable."

The unsettled feeling rose to Rachel's throat. "I don't know what you mean."

"The fact that Jack and I . . ." Loretta paused, as if searching for just the right words. "It isn't official, and we haven't set a date, but . . ."

Rachel's eyes widened and she could barely choke the words out. "You're planning to marry?"

"We've had an unspoken agreement for several years."

Rachel's heart seemed to drop somewhere in the vicinity of her toes. "I see."

"I didn't know if you'd heard anything last night . . ." Loretta tipped her head toward Jack's bedroom. "We did our best to be quiet."

Loretta's words as much as trod on Rachel's vulnerable heart. "I slept like the dead," she told Loretta, injecting a calm neutrality into her voice. "I didn't hear a thing."

Loretta swiped a hand across her brow in relief. "Thank God. It's awkward enough with you having to share with Jack, let alone to be witness to —"

The rattle of the door cut Loretta off. She turned to Jack as he entered the suite. "You're back," she said.

"They couldn't find a fax," he told her. "When did Dad say he'd send it?"

"This morning sometime," Loretta said, tossing back the thick fall of her hair. "But you know your dad, he probably forgot."

She extended a hand to Rachel. "Ready to go?"

Rachel's eyes sought out Jack's. His gaze met hers, but only briefly, then slid away. He was obviously embarrassed to have made love with his cousin when Rachel had been sleeping just a few feet away.

Loretta drove her stake even deeper when she sidled up to Jack and linked her arm with his. "Thanks for last night," she said, softly enough to be intimate, but loudly enough for Rachel to hear.

Rachel couldn't bear another moment. "I have to get my purse," she gasped as she hurried for her bedroom and closed the door behind her.

She made it to privacy just as the tears blurring her eyes tipped down onto her cheeks. Swallowing against the tightness in her throat, she gulped in air, struggling to calm herself. But nothing she did could clear the images from her mind of Jack and Loretta in each other's arms.

Stop being such an idiot, she told herself. There was nothing between herself and Jack, no reason at all that he shouldn't take up with his cousin now that she was here. Yes, Jack had kissed Rachel a few times, had seemed mildly interested in her. But that had only been because of proximity, the fact that they'd been thrown so closely together.

He had a history with Loretta, and was probably only too happy that she was here and available. Now that he had a truly beautiful woman to woo, what would he need with Rachel anymore?

Rachel picked up the glass of water she'd set on the bedside table the night before and took a quick drink. Then she refilled the glass and downed that too, as if she could wash away her tears with the cool liquid.

The water steadied her, as did the quick splash on her face. When she returned to the living area with her purse, she was actually able to plaster a smile on her face.

She saw immediately that Jack had moved away from Loretta, had shaken his arm free from hers. Rachel resolutely refused to be cheered by that fact.

"All set," she said brightly.

She ignored the concern in Jack's face, the trace of guilt she saw in Loretta's. Rachel patted the combs tucked over her ears, as if the neatness of her hair were the only issue on her mind.

"Shall we go?" she asked.

When Jack might have taken her arm to escort her from the room, she neatly sidestepped him. Glancing over her shoulder as she stepped into the hall, she saw his frown, but still, she kept her distance. Her heart was already broken. She didn't need his touch to drive the point home.

Chapter 7

I will not let it upset me.

Shifting in the makeup artist's chair, Rachel fixed her resolute gaze on the barely controlled panic around her. The busy crew hurried from one side of the restaurant to the other to complete the final details of the shoot. The set designer had taken over one booth, laying out the table setting precisely — napkin holder in perfect alignment with the table edge, tidy bottles of syrup in a neat row, forest green place mats and flatware military straight.

Since the newly built restaurant wasn't due to open for another week, it was an ideal location for a commercial taping. The mauve vinyl of the seats and pale rose tabletops were pristine. Everything was still squeaky clean, perfect under the bright, hot lights.

Rachel sighed as she observed the frenetic

activity. The scene provided a fascinating slice of life she'd never seen before, certainly ample distraction from the ache centering on her heart.

Except, of course, that the object of her anxiety sat beside her, his long legs stretched out inches from hers, his broad shoulders close enough to touch. His nearness tugged at her awareness, warred with her determined effort to be cheerful. She forced herself to keep her eyes away from Jack's lean length, gritting her teeth against the yearning inside her.

"You're creasing your foundation, love," the makeup man told her, smoothing a thumb across her forehead.

Rachel relaxed the frown from her brow, transferring her tension to her hands, locked together under the paper shawl that protected her prim, pale blue blouse. Unable to resist, she glanced at Jack sidelong, hoping her lowered lids would conceal her attention.

Jack had been the makeup man's first victim, and if his dark look was any indication, the thick cover-up probably itched him as abominably as it did her. They'd dressed him in chocolate brown slacks and a dress shirt the exact shade of Bordeaux cream. The man was too yummy by half.

The man was also already spoken for.

Rachel's narrowed gaze shifted to Loretta on the far side of the restaurant. Jack's cousin had taken charge from the moment they'd arrived, hustling Rachel and Jack into their wardrobe, then into makeup, reeling off instructions from her clipboard to cameraman and director. Just why a corporate attorney was serving as a production assistant wasn't clear, but Rachel supposed the woman would do anything to stay next to Jack.

Rachel took some cheer in the director's exasperated glare at Loretta's back as the woman marched off to her next victim. When Rachel glanced at Jack to see his reaction, he surprised her with a smile and a wink. His smile faded when Loretta turned and headed in their direction.

Rachel allowed herself the catty observation that the frothy red ruffles on Loretta's blouse arrived a full minute before she did, then reined in her uncharitable thoughts. She supposed if she had that kind of decolletage, she might wear low-cut blouses like that, too.

Loretta held her clipboard to her middle, and the pressure of her grip nearly pushed her generous breasts over the brink. Rachel kept her eyes fixed on Loretta's nose, not wanting to see Jack slaver over his cousin's cleavage the way the cameraman had.

"Did you want another look at the script?" Loretta asked, sidling closer to Jack, shoulders back so that her chest was nearly in his face.

"I only have one line," he told her, edging away. "I think I can remember it."

Loretta turned her million-watt smile on Rachel. "How about you? Have your lines memorized?"

The makeup man finished, whisking the paper shawl from Rachel so that she could step from the chair. "I think so," she told Loretta. Rachel smoothed the trim, royal blue slacks the wardrobe woman had provided, then took the mirror the makeup artist held out. She made a face at her reflection, hoping the hot lights and cameras would be kind.

"Fine," Loretta said in a clipped tone. "We need you on the set now."

Rachel flicked a quick glance at Jack, then stepped around him and headed for the table set up for the shoot. Although he kept his distance as he followed, she could feel him behind her as surely as if he touched her.

"Mr. Hanford, we'll be shooting you first," the director said as they approached.

"Then Mrs. Hanford, then the both of you together."

Although the director had only meant it figuratively, the reference to Rachel as Jack's wife sent a skitter down her spine. It was a far too pleasurable sensation, one that didn't bear thinking about.

Suppressing a threatening smile, Rachel stood back as Jack seated himself in the restaurant booth. The director shoved earphones over her head and adjusted the attached microphone. She prowled the set, making a last check of the camera angles.

Then the director called out, "Action!" and the shooting began. Any illusion Rachel might have entertained as to the glamour of working in television quickly dispersed. Jack had to say his line over and over again, his inflection changing at the director's command while the camera's lens captured each and every take.

Finally, it was her turn. Jack rose from the booth and brushed past her. She held her head high as she slipped into the booth.

When the director cued her to begin, she smiled at the camera and recited, "Right as always, Jack."

The director's "Cut!" jolted Rachel nearly out of her seat.

She turned to the woman. "What was wrong?"

"You're speaking too fast, you're too wooden, and you didn't keep your eyes on the camera," the woman told her.

"Sorry," Rachel gulped.

As the director backed away, muttering something about amateurs, Rachel raised a shaky hand to her head. Her finger tips had nearly touched her neatly styled hair when she heard a horrified gasp from the makeup man. Rachel froze, looking to Jack for support.

"If you mess up your hair, we'll have to start over," he told her.

She gave a tremulous laugh. "Yes. Of course."

"If you're ready over there?" the director called out. "Roll tape!"

This time Rachel belted out her line, stretching her mouth into a broad smile to conceal the sheer terror that lay just beneath the surface. She glanced over at the director.

"Fine," the woman said. "One more time, a little more relaxed."

The tape rolled again for another take. This time, Rachel felt considerably more relaxed. By the fifth take, she was almost enjoying herself. By the seventh, the edge of boredom had set in.

Finally the director was satisfied, and ordered the camera crew to reposition the shot. The makeup man hurried over to repair Rachel's face, fussing with her hair a moment before scurrying from the set. Rachel slumped in the booth in exhaustion.

"Can't quit now," Jack told her as he offered her a hand up from the booth. "We still have the two-shot."

Rachel let him lead her to a chair off to one side. "Have you done this before?" Rachel asked.

He took a seat next to her. "Several times. My father's had me selling pancakes one way or another since I was six." He reached over to take her hand. "How are you doing?"

Rachel stared at their linked hands, astounded that the heat generated didn't ignite them both. "Fine," she said in a breathy whisper, as all her efforts to distance herself from him melted away like warm butter.

Then he pulled away and Rachel attended to reordering her brain cells that rampaged in hormonal glee. Despite her efforts, when the director hurried over to give them their instructions, Rachel missed every other word the woman said. Something about forks, pancakes and syrup, the food stylist and a bucket.

The food stylist part Rachel understood. Rachel could see the woman positioning the last pancake on a stack of four, concentrating as intensely as an artist sculpting a masterpiece. She brushed away the stray crumbs, then used a small paintbrush to moisten the top pancake with egg white.

But what was the bucket for?

Jack took her hand again. "We'd better get back to the set."

He slipped into the booth and tugged her in after him. Rachel scrambled to remember her other line as Jack's thigh pressed against hers.

"Ready on the set," the director called out.

The food stylist scurried over to the booth with her artful creation and set it down in front of Rachel. The woman had cut a neat wedge from the stack and had carefully speared the bite with the tines of a fork. The stylist handed Rachel the fork.

"It looks too perfect to eat," Rachel said, taking the fork from the stylist.

"That's the idea," the woman said before she hurried off for Jack's plate. She returned with an exquisite arrangement of eggs, sausage and hash browns.

"The bucket's behind you," the stylist said, then walked away.

The bucket again. Rachel opened her mouth to ask Jack its purpose, but the director motioned that she was ready to begin. Rachel stored her question away for the next break.

As Rachel held her fork in a shaky hand, Jack gave her a thumbs-up under the table. Rachel dragged in a long breath and decided she just might make it through this.

"Ready for the kiss!" the director called out.

Rachel turned to Jack just as he turned to her. "Kiss?" they said in unison.

The word was drowned out by the director shouting, "Roll tape!" and Rachel snapped to attention.

"Hanford's pancakes are almost as sweet as you, Jack," she said, smiling up at him before lifting her fork to eat her bite of pancakes.

"Cut!" the director shouted before the fork reached Rachel's lips. "Where's the kiss?"

"What kiss?" Rachel asked in confusion.

"The one that comes right after your line," the director said. She motioned over her assistant and took the script from her. She pointed to the page. "It's right here."

Rachel stared at the script in the director's hand. The description after her line of dialogue read, *Mrs. Hanford kisses Mr. Hanford on the cheek.*

Loretta bustled over, snatched the page from the director. "This wasn't in our version."

The director grabbed it back. "Henry Hanford faxed this to us this morning. He insisted it be included."

"But-but-but," Loretta stuttered.

"Take two!" the director shouted, turning away from Loretta. The director's assistant politely but firmly led Jack's cousin out of camera range.

Mrs. Hanford kisses Mr. Hanford. Rachel shot a quick look at Jack and nearly dropped her fork at the intense way he was staring at her mouth. Over and over in her mind, like an endless instant replay, she saw her lips pressed against Jack's cheek.

"Roll tape!" the director called out, kicking Rachel back into gear.

Smiling brightly, Rachel belted out, "Panford's Handshakes are almost as sweet as you, Jack!"

She leaned toward Jack and nearly hit the ceiling at the director's shout of "Cut!"

She took one last look at that lovely, unkissed cheek. "What's wrong?"

"Panford's Handshakes?" Jack asked wryly.

"Oh," Rachel said, abashed.

Jack took her hand under the table. "It's just a kiss, sweetheart," he murmured.

She smiled tremulously. "A kiss is just a kiss?"

He squeezed her hand, then released it and they returned their attention to the director. This time, Rachel delivered her line perfectly, then leaned into Jack and brushed a kiss against his cheek. With a sigh, she sat back again and slipped the bite of pancake into her mouth.

And grimaced at the taste of cold flapjacks.

"Cut!" the director shouted impatiently. The woman took one step toward Rachel.

Rachel waved her off. "I know, I know," she mumbled around the mouthful of pancakes. She swallowed to clear her mouth.

Jack's eyes widened in surprise. Rachel looked at the fork, then up at him. "What?"

"The bucket," he said, as the food stylist brought Rachel another forkful of pancakes.

While the food stylist fussed, Rachel sent a questioning look Jack's way. Not the wisest of moves, because it brought her attention to the vivid blue of his eyes, something she'd been doing her best to ignore.

"Your hand is trembling," the food stylist pointed out. "Please try to control it."

"Sorry," Rachel muttered, repositioning her gaze to Jack's ear. She thought she heard him say something about the bucket again, but she knew it wouldn't do to focus too much on the timbre of his voice.

"Take two!" the director shouted, and Rachel repeated her memorized actions with determination. Recite the line, smile, kiss Jack's cheek, eat the pancakes. Prepared this time, she didn't flinch at the cold mouthful, managing to smile as she swallowed them down.

This time, not only did Jack stare at her, but several members of the crew as well. She turned to the director. "Did I have a line there?"

"Cut!" the director snarled.

"What did I do?" Rachel asked, feeling color rise in her face.

His face tilted toward the makeup artist to allow the man to brush away a sheen of sweat. "You're supposed to use the bucket."

Rachel gritted her teeth in frustration. "What bucket?"

"The spit bucket," Jack told her, gesturing behind her as the makeup man shifted his attentions to Rachel.

She wrinkled her nose at the unappetizing description and received an admonishing tap from the makeup artist's brush. She waited for the man to finish, then turned to look. A plastic bucket sat behind the booth, just out of camera range.

"Oh," she said, feeling foolish.

He laid his hand on hers. "You take the bite, give it a chew, then spit it into the bucket after the take."

"Oh," she said again, enjoying the warmth of his hand. "That's pretty yucky."

"Less yucky than twenty big bites of pancakes in a row." His fingers drifted across her knuckles. She never would have thought it possible to feel someone's fingerprints, but she felt the impression of every ridge on Jack's finger tips.

The director's booming voice jolted her hand from his. "If you're ready?"

Rachel traded forks with the food stylist, gripping the laden one until she felt the handle dig into the palm of her hand. The director signaled to roll the tape, Rachel spoke and smiled and kissed and took her bite, concentrated on one chew —

And snagged her gaze on Jack's blue eyes. The pancakes were halfway to her stomach before she realized she'd swallowed. And despite her best efforts to control her dismay, the director's call to "Cut!" informed her she hadn't succeeded.

Four more takes followed in quick succession. Each time Rachel chanted, *Chew and spit, chew and spit,* like a mantra. But each time, something about Jack's face would mesmerize her, the warmth of his cheek against her lips, the cleft in his chin. It would distract her, and at the crucial moment, she swallowed.

She gave up, finally. If she had to eat a hundred pancakes, she would, just to get a decent take so that they could all go home. And despite the queasiness that roiled in her stomach at about take eighteen, Rachel doggedly chewed and smiled her way through each attempt.

When the director yelled, "That's a take and a wrap!" after the twenty-second try, she nearly collapsed to the table in relief. As it was, her trembling legs nearly gave way when she got to her feet.

Jack immediately cupped her elbow with his hand. "Are you okay?"

Could a pancake overdose make your head spin? she wondered. Or was it because Jack was standing so close to her?

"I think I need to lie down," she whispered faintly.

Jack urged her across the studio. "Let's let the makeup man clean you up, then I'll drive you back to the hotel."

She nodded woozily. She sank into the

makeup artist's chair, then had to grip Jack's hand when the scent of cold cream warred with the flapjacks in her stomach. She bit hard on the tip of her tongue to counteract the pressure in the back of her throat.

What followed was a bit of a blur. She remembered changing clothes, then Jack helping her into the front seat of the car. She vaguely recalled his hands resting on her shoulders as he led her across the hotel lobby. Then there was a foggy image of him in her bedroom, filling her vision as he tucked her into her bed.

Then he was gone, and she only just made it to the bathroom before the consequence of her overindulgence hit. Afterward, she rinsed her mouth, brushed her teeth, and slipped out of the blouse and skort before staggering back to the bed.

Then the previous sleepless night conspired with her stomach's rebellion, and Rachel drifted off, exhausted.

Jack stood in the doorway of Rachel's bedroom, a glass of ginger ale in his hand, and watched Rachel sleeping. Her lips were parted slightly, and her soft exhalations stirred the silk of her golden hair. She had the innocent look of a child asleep, yet the tantalizing glimpse of her bare shoulder stirred him as no child would.

He'd entered the room and crossed halfway to the bed before he even realized he'd moved. He stopped short, rattled by his automatic response to her. The splash of ginger ale on his fingers drew his gaze to his trembling hand. He glared at Rachel's sleeping form, almost as angry at her as at himself for his overreaction to her.

Moving with deliberation, he set the glass on the night table beside the bed, then headed for the bathroom to rinse off the sticky stuff. He gazed at her through the bathroom door as he dried his hands. She lay with her back to him, the light blanket tucked up under her arm.

His eyes followed the lines of her slender shoulder, then the dip of her waist and the swell of her hip. His brain sent an all-too-explicit image of his hand tracing that same path in a leisurely exploration.

He shook his head to clear the tantalizing picture. Lord, had he turned into some kind of lech who got his jollies ogling sleeping women? He damn well ought to get out of there and leave Rachel alone.

He tossed the towel aside and dragged his gaze from Rachel. With determined strides, he headed for the bedroom door, keeping even his peripheral vision directed forward. He'd leave her be, let her sleep off her discomfort.

What if she has a fever?

Ridiculous, he told himself as he gripped the doorjamb, his back to the bedroom. She'd eaten too much and it made her sick to her stomach.

But what if it's something else? What if she really needs you?

It was testimony to his fogged brain that he was so easily convinced. He turned slowly on his heel and crept to the side of the bed as if he hadn't been stomping around in there the last ten minutes. Eyeing the narrow bit of mattress between Rachel's back and the edge of the bed, he perched there beside her, keeping a slim gap between their bodies.

A gap she immediately closed by snuggling close to him. Now her body curved around him, her back pressed against his thigh, her round, soft bottom warming his hip. It was all he could do not to sweep a hand across her body, to dip his fingers into her dark, warm secrets.

Gritting his teeth, Jack forced himself to place only a chaste wrist against her brow. As he'd suspected, her flesh was warm, but not hot; she had no fever. He made to move his hand away, would have, in fact, if she hadn't moved her head to cradle her cheek in his hand.

Now he could no more move his palm from her soft lips than he could stop breathing. The feel of her lips brushing against him nearly stole the breath clean from his body, not to mention wreaking havoc with his heart. Then her fingers crept up to curl around his wrist, and his hammering heart kicked his breathing back into gear, at a much higher rate than had to be healthy.

When she planted a moist kiss in the center of his palm, he could feel his heart straining against his chest. He made a virtuous attempt to tug his hand free, certain she had acted in her sleep. He swallowed back a groan when she brushed her lips again against his sensitive skin, reminding himself that Rachel's conscious mind was unaware of what she was doing.

But then her eyes fluttered open. Her gaze slanted up at him, and for a moment, he saw her confusion. He waited for her to pull away, to sit bolt upright in indignation. But her eyes drifted shut.

And she kissed him again.

It was too much. He cupped his free hand under her head, threading his fingers through her honey-blonde hair. She turned to look up at him, confusion gone from her gaze, replaced by a smoky light. A faint smile curved her lips and that was all the encouragement Jack needed.

He dipped his head until only the warmth of their lips brushed, then dipped again to make a first fleeting contact. The breath of her sigh mingled with his, urging him to taste her. A compulsion to thrust his tongue into her mouth gripped him and he dragged in a lungful of air to resist.

Moving slowly, he stretched out beside her, the thin blanket that covered her the only barrier between them. She turned to face him, one thigh brushing briefly against his throbbing erection. He swallowed against the sweet pain of that contact, focusing instead on the feel of her cheek against his palm, the smoky hazel of her eyes meeting his.

"Rachel," he whispered. He touched a kiss to her brow, to her temples, to the bridge of her nose. Her fluttering lashes stroked his cheek and he brushed his lips against them, kissing her eyes closed.

"Jack?"

The little catch in her sleepy voice sent a shaft of sensation straight down his spine. He moved his hand along her slender back, pressing her against him, at once frustrated and relieved to have the thin blanket in his way.

He felt her hand move tentatively along his side, her finger tips skimming the smooth broadcloth of his shirt. Her shy touch left a trail of fire on his flesh.

"We weren't supposed to touch each other," he whispered.

Her gaze fixed on his. "I know."

He moved his mouth close to hers. "I want to taste you," he said softly.

A part of him prayed that she would refuse him, that her hands on his body would push him away. When he'd kissed her before, the inappropriateness of the time and place had reined him in. Each time, the situation had been quite public, giving him an automatic safety net.

But here, in the intimacy of her room, her bed, he could explore her sweetness without restraint. They could take a kiss as far as they chose, even to its inevitable conclusion.

"Please," she said softly.

Rachel tipped her head up slightly in invitation, and destroyed his hope that she would be the one to draw the line. It was up to him to resist or surrender.

One taste — he could be satisfied with that. Then he would do the noble thing and drag himself away from her.

Jack feathered his lips against hers, once, twice. When she parted her lips with a sigh, he ran the tip of his tongue along the softness of her mouth. She strained against him, her own tongue sliding briefly against his.

He plunged deeper into her mouth, sweeping into the sensitive recesses. He swallowed her moan and tightened his fingers at her waist, tugging her even closer.

Her hand moved restlessly down his body, her nails grazing the musculature of his back, sending jolts of sensation through him. He deepened the kiss even further, his fingers tangled in her hair, cradling her head.

Her hand came to rest at his hip, and every other thought was blasted out of his mind by the image of her palm moving lower to press against him. He realized he teetered on a razor's edge, one he sensed he understood more than she. Rachel might think they could continue, take another step without falling from the precipice. But he knew better.

His hand shot down to capture hers, to bring it to safety. Then he dragged in a long breath and levered himself up to sit beside her. He shifted away from her and readjusted his slacks.

"How are you?" he asked, his back to her.

"Okay," she answered in a small voice.

Marvelous. Now he'd upset her. His erratic behavior — pawing her one moment, pulling away the next — must have her thoroughly confused.

He rose, turning to face her. "Rachel —" he began.

She scooted away from him, clutching the blanket to her. One bra strap slipped from a bare shoulder. "I'm fine," she said. "My stomach's fine. A little more rest and I'll be great."

He shoved his hands into his pockets, feeling like a heel. "I don't suppose you're eager for dinner."

She grimaced. "Not any time soon. You go ahead." She slanted him a quick glance. "I'm sure Loretta would go with you."

Loretta! He'd left her at the restaurant. He'd been so concerned about getting Rachel back to the hotel he'd forgotten entirely about his cousin.

He scraped his fingers through his hair. "I'd better call." He headed for the door. "Maybe one of the crew gave her a ride."

"Don't worry about me," Rachel called out. "You two go on to dinner without me."

Setting his teeth against the wobble in Rachel's voice, Jack dialed the restaurant. He'd have to go back in and talk to Rachel, apologize, make things right somehow. But as he was listening with half an ear to Loretta's angry harangue, the door to Rachel's bedroom swung shut. Before he could stretch the phone cord across the kitchen, he heard of the soft click of the lock.

He cut off Loretta's tirade with a promise to come pick her up, then hung up the phone. But when he knocked on Rachel's door, first gently, then more insistently, he got no answer.

He stood there for several moments more, tamping back the urge to batter the door off its hinges. Then with a growl of frustration, he snatched up his car keys and left the suite to pick up Loretta.

Rachel waited until she heard the suite door shut before tossing aside the blanket and scrambling from the bed. A quick glance at the bedside clock showed her it was a little past six. She couldn't bear to just lie here for several hours, imagining Jack and his cousin together, picturing him kissing Loretta as he had her . . .

The heat of remembered passion blasted through her body, chased by the shivering chill of mortification. How could she have thrown herself at Jack, all but *offered* herself to him the way she had? No doubt he'd been concerned and had only come to check on her. But his touch had overwhelmed her. Suddenly she was pawing him and snuggling up against him like a cat in heat.

Yes, he'd taken what she'd thrown in his lap, but soon enough his better sense had reasserted itself. And all it took was one mention of Loretta to remind him where his true interest lay. And to remind Rachel just how foolish she'd been.

She had to get out, find something to distract her for the evening. She snatched up the phone to request a cab from the front desk, then threw on jeans and sweater and made a stab at ordering her hair. She dithered over writing a note to Jack, then felt it only fair he know she wasn't spirited away by aliens.

She made it to the waiting taxi with only moments to spare. Just as the cabbie drove off, Jack's car pulled up to the hotel lobby. Rachel couldn't help herself; she turned to peer out the back window of the taxi and watched as Jack rounded the car to open Loretta's door. Rachel saw Loretta place her hand in Jack's just before the cab turned a corner and cut off her view.

"Where to?" the cabbie asked as he pulled into traffic.

Good question. Her escape plan had included everything but a destination. Her stomach still rebelled against food, so dinner was out. She rubbed at her temples as the cabbie waited for the light with one eye on her in the rearview mirror.

"I'd like to see a movie," she said at last. "Where's the closest theater?"

"That revival house up the road plays the classics," the cabbie answered.

"What's showing?" she asked as the light turned green and the cabbie moved forward.

"*The African Queen,*" he told her.

Her stomach clenched. "I want to see a new movie," she said tightly.

The cabbie nodded as he cut into traffic to turn left. "The Cinema Six it is."

As the cab zipped along the highway, Rachel breathed deeply to ease the ache inside her. She only needed a few more minutes, she decided. Then her natural optimism would return.

But the image of a certain witchy brunette dug at her like a bit of gravel in her shoe, making cheer a hopeless prospect. Loretta, reaching up to Jack. Loretta, placing her hand so intimately in his.

Rachel glowered out the window at the swiftly passing scenery. There darn well better be a comedy playing at the theater. Not that she knew whether she wanted to laugh, or cry.

Chapter 8

Jack checked Rachel's empty room a second time, peeking into the bathroom, shaking off the temptation to look under her bed. But he couldn't deny that she was gone.

He felt faint comfort that her clothes were still there. In all likelihood, she hadn't run back home. So where the hell was she?

"She left a note."

He spun on his heel to see Loretta standing in the doorway of Rachel's bedroom with the pad of hotel paper in her hand. Jack covered the distance to the door in two long strides and snatched the pad from Loretta's hand.

I went out.

Three little words that said everything and told nothing. Jack waved the pad at Loretta.

"What does she mean, she went out?" he demanded of his cousin.

A brief flicker of guilt in her eyes, then she tipped up her chin indignantly. "It means, she went out."

Jack glared at her another moment, then back down at the pad. The brief bit of script flowed across the page, the cursive as graceful and well-shaped as the woman who'd written it. Her signature, though, seemed a bit shaky, as if her hand had trembled when she wrote it.

A sudden thought rocketed into his brain. "Oh, my God," he muttered.

Loretta tugged at his arm. "What?"

He gestured with the tablet. "She wrote this under duress. Someone *forced* her to write this."

"What are you talking about?"

He stabbed a finger at the message. "Kidnappers. They came in here, forced a pen into her hand and —"

"You're nuts!" Loretta exclaimed.

"Or a burglar." He slapped the pad against the kitchen counter. "He planned to rob the place, discovered Rachel —"

Loretta grabbed his arm. "Jack, you've gone off the deep end. Next you'll be saying aliens abducted her."

He rounded on her and for the teensiest moment, her suggestion sounded almost plausible. Then he threw the pad across the room, angry with his own ludicrous imagination.

"Where the hell did she go?" he asked.

"Just out, Jack," Loretta said softly. "She probably just needed some time to herself."

He knew damn well why. He'd driven her off, with his hot and cold treatment of her. One moment he couldn't keep his hands off her, the next he was pushing her away. She was probably damned confused.

Loretta's gentle touch on his arm brought his attention back to her. "I think I might have had something to do with her leaving."

He immediately grasped for something that might assuage his own guilt. "What do you mean?"

Loretta suddenly found the carpet fascinating. "I told her something that might have upset her."

Jack tipped Loretta's chin up. "What?"

To her credit, she kept her gaze on him. "That you and I were getting married."

"Why in the world did you tell her that?" he blurted, then could have kicked himself when he saw the hurt in her eyes.

She looked away again, "I wanted her to back off. I knew what she was beginning to mean to you."

"She doesn't mean anything to me," he

said, the quick denial suspicious even to his own ears.

Loretta gazed up at him wryly. "Yeah, right."

He sighed. "I love you, Loretta. I cherish our friendship. But marriage —"

She shrugged, although he saw the hurt in her gray eyes. "Can't blame a girl for wishful thinking."

He'd done enough wishful thinking lately about Rachel that he understood completely. And what he'd done earlier — she had to think he was a total jerk to be kissing her when he was engaged to another woman.

He dragged a hand through his hair. "I've got to find her, Loretta."

She nodded. "I'd like to help. I've always been a glutton for punishment."

He grinned and gave her a one-armed hug. Then he grabbed the phone and dialed the front desk.

Shivering a little in the late evening chill, Rachel waved to the cabbie as he pulled up to the cineplex outside the mall. As she climbed inside the cab, she tried to blink away the burning in her eyes, a consequence of sitting through four hours of back-to-back movies.

After sitting through the first film, a raucous comedy that the rest of the audience had found hilarious, Rachel still couldn't bear to return to the hotel. So she stood in line again for a big-name action-adventure film that her sisters had insisted was the best movie of the year.

She supposed ordinarily she would have enjoyed the nail-biting tension of the second film, but an uneasy ache still lodged squarely in her stomach. Nothing could have soothed that nagging pain.

It was well past eleven when the taxi returned her to the hotel. She girded herself for the worst as she rode the elevator up to the suite — Jack and Loretta in a clinch on the living room couch, or their voices mingling behind the closed door of Jack's bedroom.

But somehow, what she did find — the suite empty, Jack's rumpled bed visible through the open door of his room — was even more crushing. Now she had to deal with wondering where they were and what they were doing.

Those images plagued her as she stood in the shower, as she readied herself for bed. They persisted as she huddled under the covers. They haunted her for a good long time before she finally surrendered to a restless sleep.

Jack paced the length of the living room, pausing to glare at Rachel's door when his track brought him abreast of it. Brilliant morning sunlight cut through the window, casting butter-yellow puddles on the floor. He didn't have to look at his watch to know that if she didn't emerge from the bedroom soon, they'd be late for their noontime appointment.

He'd managed to shave with a steady enough hand this morning — only three nicks along his jaw. But whatever effort he'd made to tidy his hair had been lost the first time he raked his fingers through it.

When he and Loretta couldn't immediately ascertain where Rachel had gone last night, he'd very nearly panicked. They'd determined she'd ridden off in a cab, but the cabbie had a faulty radio and hadn't reported her destination. So there was no telling where in the city she'd gone.

After an hour of fruitless calls, Loretta brought dinner up to the suite and all but force-fed him. He couldn't have said what he ate, nor exactly when Loretta left. He just looked around sometime around ten and realized she'd gone. He'd laid down after that, thinking foolishly that he might make the time move faster by sleeping. But twenty minutes of thrashing around had him on his feet again.

He retrieved his car and drove the nearby streets, his eyes scanning the sidewalks for Rachel. He even circled the parking lot of the nearby mall, dithering over whether he should go inside. But the shops closed at ten, so it was unlikely she was still there.

He caught sight of a police car as he headed back to the hotel and the sudden skittering thought of reporting Rachel missing entered, then fled his mind. He had no real reason to think something had happened to her and the police wouldn't even be interested for at least another day.

Relief swamped him when he returned to the suite and found her bedroom door shut. When he pressed his ear to the door, he heard the shower running, then the sound of the water cut off. He raised his hand to knock, intent on finding out where the hell she'd gone. But he realized his ragged emotions would only drive him to say things he shouldn't.

So he'd gone quietly to his own suite and shut himself inside. He had no hope for sleep, but at least he could lie in the dark room secure that Rachel had returned safely.

He couldn't help a quick glance at his

watch. If not for the phone call from his father this morning, he would have called the radio station that had arranged their noontime commitment and asked to have it shifted back another hour. He'd just as soon Rachel get all the sleep she wanted.

He'd just as soon never have to face her this morning. He'd just as soon batter down the door and join her in the bed.

He shook the confusion from his head and tried to focus on the problem his father had presented him with this morning. An employee they'd long suspected of corporate spying had finally been caught in the act. His father wanted him in Chicago to handle the press.

Which meant he had to get through this luncheon engagement with Rachel in a timely fashion so that he could take off for the corporate office. It also meant that for the day and a half the messy business would likely take, he'd be without her.

Irritated at the lonely feeling that bloomed in the wake of that thought, he strode to Rachel's door and raised his fist to pound on it. Before he could make contact, it opened.

Eyeing his raised fist, Rachel jumped back a step. "Oh! Good morning."

"Where were you?" he demanded without preamble.

"I left a note." She tried to dodge past him.

Jack grabbed her ann, far more tightly than he should have. A trace of fear flickered across her face. Taking a breath, he let go, struggling to control the anger that had followed in the wake of his fear. "Last night," he said a shade more gently. "Where were you?"

"At the movies," she answered, then she opened the door wider and slipped past him.

He dogged her as she crossed to the kitchen cupboard. "All night long?"

Rachel pulled out a glass and filled it from the tap. "I saw two."

"Anything to stay away from me."

He'd meant it as an observation, maybe an apology of sorts. But it came out as an accusation, its bitterness shocking him.

She turned to him, the glass trembling in her hand. "I needed time to myself."

"I'm sorry," he said, not entirely sure for what, but hoping the apology would encompass all his sins.

Her gaze dipped to the glass as she took a sip. "There's nothing to be sorry for."

Jack stilled her hand before she could take another drink. "There is one thing." He waited until her gaze tipped up to his. "I shouldn't have kissed you last night."

A tumult of emotions washed across her face, foremost confusion and hurt. "No, you shouldn't have."

"Not for the reason you think," he said, his fingers still overlaying hers on the glass.

Her confusion deepened. "What do you mean?"

"There's nothing between Loretta and me," he told her. "No intimacy, no marriage plans. She's a dear friend and nothing more." He saw the brief flare of hope in Rachel's eyes and knew he had to squelch it. "But —"

"But?" Rachel prodded.

"But I have no intention of ever marrying. Ever," he added emphatically. "And a woman like you . . ."

"A woman like me?" she prompted.

"You deserve a man who can make a commitment. An unselfish man. One who can love you." His heart twanged at the word "love."

Her gaze narrowed on him. "And so you shouldn't have kissed me."

"Absolutely not."

"Because if we'd gone any further . . ." She jerked her hand away and slammed the sloshing glass on the counter. ". . . if we'd made love, God forbid, I might have gotten all googly-eyed afterward and expected some kind of commitment from you."

He backed away a step. "Yes, well, no. What I mean is . . ."

Rachel advanced, one finger poking him in the chest. "And since you know ever so much more about me than I do, *you* decided what was best for me."

"Yes, I mean, no, I mean . . ." He juggled his thoughts, trying to unscramble them. What had he meant?

"Did it ever occur to you, Jack Hanford," she said with a decisive poke of her finger, "that I might have the good sense to realize you weren't the marrying kind and I might choose to go to bed with you anyway?"

He gulped, both at the depth of her fury and the prospect that maybe he could have slept with her without the threat of entanglements. Sharp guilt immediately plunged through him at the ignoble thought.

"I assumed —"

"You assumed!" she snapped.

"I assumed that as someone with less experience, you would appreciate —"

"What makes you think I'm inexperienced?" she asked, chin tipped up in challenge. If it weren't for the wash of pink across her cheeks, he might have believed her bravado.

Now he was truly caught. Because if he

told her that her shy touch, her tentative explorations, her naive openness had all but broadcast her lack of experience, he knew she'd be completely mortified. Yet it was her response to the newness of lovemaking that aroused him past reasoning.

Jack shrugged, hoping nothing in his thoughts showed in his face. "I guessed."

Another moment of bluster, then Rachel backed away. "Well, you don't know everything," she muttered, and grabbed the glass to dump its contents in the sink. "What do we have scheduled today?"

Uneasy at her capitulation, he forced his thoughts to their morning appointment. "A brunch. If we leave immediately, we should just make it."

She moved past him, taking exaggerated care not to touch him. "Let me grab my purse."

He couldn't quite let her go. "Did you pack?"

She stopped at the end of the counter. "Yes."

"Because we leave this afternoon."

"I know. I'm all packed." She headed for her room again.

"I'll just make a phone call, then." He made a show of picking up the phone and punching out a number.

"Who are you calling?" she asked, hesitating in the door of her bedroom.

"Loretta. She was worried sick about you last night." He felt a peculiar satisfaction at the guilty flush that colored Rachel's face. "Tell her I'm sorry." She ducked inside her bedroom.

She hadn't told *him* she was sorry, he thought sourly. Then Loretta answered and he let her know about Rachel, that she was fine, that she'd only gone out to the movies. He said good-bye, as well, since they wouldn't be seeing her again.

When Rachel reappeared, they headed downstairs to the car. In the elevator, he took advantage of their solitude to look at her, to admire the way she looked in the hip-length gold sweater tunic and matching stirrup pants. She'd accented the sweater with an unusual polished wood and gold necklace that nestled between her breasts.

He turned away as the elevator opened, annoyed that as simple a thing as a necklace could lead his thoughts astray. But as much as he might try to bat the image aside, he kept picturing Rachel in his bed wearing nothing but that necklace and a smile just for him.

Jack strode ahead of her to the desk to close out their bill. He arranged to have their luggage brought down so that they could pick it up after their brunch. He had to get down to the local airport by four and so had no time to waste.

When they reached the car, he opened the door for her, standing behind it to hide his reaction to her. He nearly reached out to help her into the car, then thrust his hand into the pocket of his gray slacks. The less contact he had with her, the better.

He rounded the car and climbed in. She tugged on her seat belt and Jack found himself mesmerized by the way the shoulder strap crossed between her breasts. He shook his head to clear it and started the car.

"I can't remember — who's scheduled for brunch today?" Rachel asked as they pulled out of the parking lot.

"Mr. and Mrs. Willens," he said as he navigated the traffic. "They won a local radio contest. Brunch with Mr. and Mrs. Hanford."

"At the Hanford House of Pancakes, I suppose."

"Of course." He eased onto I-64 and headed toward the mall. "You might want to pass on the pancakes this morning."

She laughed, a beautiful sound, and the tension from the previous night and the morning dissolved. He glanced over at her, and captured a brief snapshot of her smile, the light in her eyes, the glimmer of gold in her hair.

Something turned over in his chest, a trembling, a tiny earthquake that shook him to the core. And although he'd looked away, had returned his focus to the road and his driving, he felt his foundations slip away.

He might be able to resist kissing Rachel, might even resist making love to her. But what had just passed between them was as inevitable as breathing the air she breathed, and far more bonding, far more binding.

Suddenly commitment didn't seem like such a dirty word anymore.

Who do I think I'm kidding? Rachel wondered as she stepped through the door of the Hanford House of Pancakes that Jack held open for her. *Making myself out to be some woman of the world. Jack didn't believe me for a minute.*

What had she hoped to accomplish anyway by implying she was experienced? That Jack would give in and make love to her, secure that she was as willing as he to love 'em and leave 'em? He'd have found out otherwise at the crucial moment and hated her for misleading him.

Not that he'd believed her anyway. She'd

seen the look in his eyes, the polite smile. She knew how awkward and clumsy she'd been with Jack. He'd only been too nice to say so.

She'd had few opportunities to improve her finesse in the bedroom. Men had only to look at her to realize she wasn't worth the trouble. She should be glad Jack was so up-front with her.

She pasted a courteous smile on her face as she shook hands with the Willenses and made the right noises when Jack introduced them. As they moved off toward their table, her stomach roiled at the thought of having to eat.

The Willenses sat next to each other on one side of the table, leaving the other two chairs for Jack and Rachel. Rachel pulled out her chair before Jack could, not wanting to risk contact with him.

When they were seated, Mr. Willens grinned at Rachel, the lines in his sixty-something face crinkling. "I understand you two are newlyweds."

"Georgie and I," Mrs. Willens said, gazing fondly at her husband, "will have been married for thirty-eight years this June."

"Wouldn't trade a minute," Mr. Willens said, rapping his knuckles on the table. "So where was it you two got married?"

Rachel's jaw dropped and she quickly snapped it shut. She smiled at the Willenses. "Could you excuse us a moment?"

She pushed back her chair and gave Jack's arm a poke. They threaded their way through the crowded tables toward the register.

She stood close to Jack so no one else could hear. "I thought people knew we weren't really married."

He shrugged. "The restaurant managers all do. They knew at the commercial shoot and the BigMart."

She looked back over her shoulder at the Willenses. They both smiled and waved. "Maybe they're just playing along."

Jack rubbed the back of his neck. "Somehow, I don't think so."

Rachel worried her lower lip with her teeth. "So what do we do?"

Jack's mouth curved into a faint smile. "Shall we decide where we got married?"

She scowled at him, then shot another glance at the contented Willenses. "Fine. Where was it?"

"Chicago?"

"I've never been to Chicago."

"How could you never have been to Chicago?"

"Could we not argue about this now?"

Rachel said impatiently.

"Fine," he said. "Your home town, then. At a church?"

She shook her head. "The Town Hall. A small wedding, with just family and a few friends."

"Great." He took her shoulders and turned her back toward the Willenses. "Let's go."

This time she let him seat her, still feeling the imprint of his hands on her shoulders. She smiled at Mr. Willens. "You were saying?"

"Just wondering where you two lovebirds got married," he said, pushing back a lock of sparse sandy hair that had slipped down his brow.

Jack leaned toward her to lay his arm across the back of her chair. "Blue Hills. Rachel's home town."

"We've been through there, Georgie," Mrs. Willens exclaimed. "Three summers ago, when we went to visit Robbie."

"Our oldest," Mr. Willens supplied. "Must be tough spending your honeymoon on a tour like this."

Jack cleared his throat and snatched his arm from her chair. No doubt remembering last night and how easily they could have made this a real honeymoon.

"It's not so bad," Rachel said. "We stay in

the best hotels, have a chance to travel a bit."

"Not much privacy, though," Mrs. Willens said.

Mr. Willens pressed a kiss on his wife's cheek. "We sure like our privacy since the kids have flown the coop."

Mrs. Willens tittered. "So where do you two go next?"

"Poseyville," Rachel said. "We start our Indiana appearances there tomorrow."

Mrs. Willens smiled brightly. "We live just outside Poseyville."

"Garden spot of Indiana," Mr. Willens said, rapping the table again with a quick one-two.

"We were so glad to see a Hanford House of Pancakes go up right in our backyard," Mrs. Willens said. "Will you be there long?"

"Two days —"

"I forgot to tell you," Jack said, placing his hand over hers on the table.

She stared at his large hand covering hers, fighting the curl of heat that centered low in her body. If she pulled her hand free, the Willenses would notice, might comment on it. But if she didn't, she doubted her brain would ever make sense of the rest of what Jack was saying.

She dragged her gaze up to him. "What's that?"

"I said, I have to go to Chicago," he repeated.

Disappointment bloomed within her. "Oh."

"Only until tomorrow," he said, patting her hand before pulling his away. "There's a bit of business I have to handle."

She dropped her hand in her lap, rubbing the sudden chill away with her fingers. "I see."

Mr. Willens took a sip of his coffee, then gestured with it at Jack, sloshing a bit on the table. "I suppose you're taking the little wife with you."

The bubble of hope in her chest burst at Jack's quick, emphatic, "No." He took a gulp of his own coffee. "I have too much work to do."

The irritation in his tone puzzled her. Was he still angry that she'd gone out last night? Or with their argument this morning? Was that why he seemed so eager to get away from her?

Rachel tipped up her chin, determined to not react to his anger. "I'll be fine. I'll go on to Poseyville without you."

He glowered at her, his jaw tensing as he looked down at her. "You'd be bored if you came to Chicago."

"I've never been to Chicago," she reminded him.

"I'll only be there one day. You'd scarcely have time to see the city before we'd have to return."

"Fine. I'll go on alone, as I said."

He scowled. "Alone?"

"Yes," she told him. "As in, by myself."

He frowned. "But I don't want you to go to the hotel alone."

She peered up at him, wondering where his sudden protectiveness came from. Was this attentive husband act all for the Willens' benefit? "I'm sure I'll be perfectly fine."

He shook his head and ran a hand over his face. "I hadn't thought about you being alone," he muttered. "Just that I wouldn't have to . . ."

"Wouldn't have to what?"

He ignored her. "Maybe I ought to bring you with me. Get a second ticket — no, that flight was booked. But there must be another out of Mount Vernon . . ."

Rachel stared at him, more and more confused. First he was adamant that she not accompany him to Chicago, now he seemed just as frantic that she should.

"I'd really rather not, Jack, if it would be so much trouble."

He didn't even seem to hear her. "I could have Dad send down the private plane. But by the time they do the flight check and refuel, it would be nearly midnight."

"Jack!" She grabbed his arm and shook it. "Listen to me."

"I could cancel," he said thoughtfully. "No, I can't, I definitely can't."

Rachel looked helplessly at the Willenses. Mr. Willens grinned. "Man, he's got it bad."

Mrs. Willens giggled prettily. "We really ought to lend a helping hand, Georgie."

The older couple exchanged a loving glance, then Mr. Willens banged on the table again. "See here, Mr. Hanford. I think we have a solution."

Jack glared at Mr. Willens. "What?"

"The little lady can just stay with us for the night," Mr. Willens said.

"We own a lovely little bed and breakfast inn," Mrs. Willens said.

"Four cozy rooms, all of them *en suite*." Mr. Willens said.

Mrs. Willens tittered. "That means they have their own bathroom."

"We'd take good care of her," said Mr. Willens.

Rachel lifted one brow at Jack, looking to him to answer. He seemed to struggle for a response.

"Well," he said.

Mr. Willens knock-knock-knocked on the

table. "It's settled, then. We'll bring the little lady home with us."

Rachel could have laughed at Jack's befuddled expression. Control of the situation had been neatly wrested from his hands by the gregarious Willenses. She smiled across the table at the older woman.

"Thank you so much," she said. "I look forward to visiting with you."

After a moment's hesitation, Jack echoed her thanks. Then the waitress appeared to take their orders. Shortly after their food arrived, a photographer from the local paper showed up and snapped endless shots of Mr. and Mrs. Hanford sharing a meal with the contest winners.

After they'd finished, the Willenses followed them to the hotel to collect Rachel's luggage. When it came time to say good-bye to Jack, the Willenses moved off a few paces to give them privacy. No doubt, they expected a passionate good-bye kiss — after all, these were newlyweds parting for the first time.

But Jack had already made it clear that he felt that kissing her was a bad mistake. It would only lead her into expectations that he had no intention of fulfilling.

So, as he gazed down at her, his eyes hot and intense, Rachel decided he was still angry with her. And when he lowered his head to hers, she assumed he intended to brush a quick peck on her cheek, a show of affection for the benefit of the Willenses. Then, when his mouth covered hers, and her world began to spin, she figured he would make his kiss as brief as possible to still keep up the illusion for the older couple.

But then his tongue slipped past her lips and thrust into her mouth. His intimate caress went on and on, driving honeyed heat straight through her, melting her middle, weakening her knees. His hand splayed across the small of her back, pressing her closer, ever closer.

He nearly stumbled when he backed away. And when she looked at him, she saw now he was truly angry. He gave the Willenses an abrupt nod of farewell, then stalked off to his car without a backward glance.

Her body still trembling in reaction, her insides turning in confusion, she watched him gun his engine and tear out of the parking lot. What in the world had she done this time?

Mrs. Willens sighed, drawing Rachel's attention to the woman's wistful smile. Mr. Willens grinned. "Ain't love grand?" he said with a chortle, then waved them both to his car.

Chapter 9

Jack stared down the length of the conference table and tried to focus on what Khosrow from marketing was saying. Jack knew it was crucial to restructure their marketing strategies after the arrest of the corporate spy. He understood how tenuous their position was, not knowing which of their future plans had been revealed and which had not.

But nothing Khosrow said made sense. How could it when the marketing director's words competed in Jack's mind with images of Rachel?

Jack rubbed at his eyes. He ought to at least make a show of paying attention. Khosrow and his team had put a great deal of effort into their alternative marketing plan. It wasn't their fault that Jack saw Rachel's lovely face on each of the hundred and fifty neatly bound pages of their report.

"So what do you think, Jack?" Khosrow asked in his soft Turkish accent.

Jack stared at the marketing director, as an erotic image of Rachel freeze-framed in his brain. He squeezed his eyes shut a moment, trying to shake off the fantasy.

"I know what you can do, Khosrow," Jack said, going for a generic response. "If you believe in that approach, I know it will be good for Hanford's."

Khosrow smiled, obviously pleased with the vote of confidence. Jack would have given anything to know just what the hell he'd just shown his confidence in.

Around the table, the marketing staff shuffled papers, gathering up reports and stuffing them into portfolios. As Henry Hanford threaded his way through the departing crowd toward Jack, his father's assistant, Moira, collected the coffee mugs and leftovers from the pastry tray she'd brought in. She frowned as she picked up Jack's uneaten bagel, then exchanged a quick look with his father.

Some silent message passed between them, and Moira met Henry's grin with a smug expression. Jack had an uneasy sensation that they knew something he didn't, but he hadn't the vaguest idea what it could be.

Henry stepped up and clapped him on the

shoulder. "Looks like we'll be coming out of this okay."

Jack tucked the marketing report into his briefcase. "It helps that Moira reported her suspicions as soon as she did."

Henry gazed at his attractive, fiftyish assistant as she piled the last of the mugs and trash on the tray. "Yes, she is a treasure, isn't she?"

A bit of color rose in Moira's cheeks as she fussed with the thermal coffeepots. Henry's eyes softened as he watched her, his face creasing into a fond smile.

A warning bell went off in Jack's head. His father and Moira? She'd been his assistant for more than twenty years, half of that time as a widow. After all these years of chasing younger women, could it be his father had finally realized the value of a woman his age?

"So how's Rachel?" his father asked, giving him a nudge.

So busy contemplating what his father's relationship with Moira might be, the question caught Jack off guard. Rachel's spoken name brought to mind immediate images of her and the pang in his chest at their separation sharpened.

"She's fine, I suppose," Jack said, focusing on the latch of his briefcase as if it held the secrets of the universe.

"You suppose?"

Jack aligned the three tumblers of the briefcase lock with scientific precision. "She was fine when I left her yesterday."

"You haven't spoken with her since?" Henry rocked back on his heels as if appalled by his son's action. "You leave her with total strangers, then you don't even have the decency to call her?"

He heard a little humph from Moira and guilt tightened inside Jack. Then irritation followed on its heels at his compulsion to explain himself to them. "I wouldn't say the Willenses were *total* strangers. They seemed like nice folks —"

"Nice folks or not," his father said, poking a finger in Jack's chest, "if you'd learned even a jot of the courtesy I've tried to drill into you over the years, you would have called her last night to make sure she'd gotten settled."

Jack backed away from his father's prodding finger. "I did call," he muttered, staring at his toes.

Henry's eyes narrowed on him. "You just said —"

"I called the Willenses, okay?" Jack said, turning to his father. "They said she was fine, I took them at their word. I didn't have to talk to Rachel."

His father glared at him a moment more, then his face eased into a smile. "That's good, then. At least you asked after her."

Something more passed between his father and Moira and an uneasiness settled in Jack's gut again. What bit of intelligence were they keeping from him? What did they know that he didn't?

Henry picked up a thick file folder from the table. "Ready to go over the financials?"

Jack glanced at his watch. Nearly noon. He made a mental calculation of the time it would take, between air travel to Mount Vernon and the drive from there to Poseyville. If he wanted to get himself and Rachel to their hotel by a decent hour, he ought to leave Hartford's Chicago headquarters by three.

"Ready as I'll ever be," he said finally. If he couldn't focus on Khosrow's marketing report, he didn't have a prayer of concentrating on his father's financials. But he might as well give it his best shot.

As he passed Moira on his way out of the conference room, Jack caught a glimpse of her contented smile. He wanted to peg her happiness on whatever was brewing between her and Henry. But his father's wink and thumbs-up disabused him of that notion.

They were playing him like a puppet, but for the life of him, he didn't know how.

Rachel nibbled at her ham sandwich, feeling a twinge of guilt that her appetite didn't match Mrs. Willens's artfully prepared lunch. The older woman's arrangement of sandwich, dill pickle and carrot curls looked like something out of a restaurant magazine.

The delicious meal should have sparked more interest in Rachel than it did. But only one topic seemed to hold Rachel's interest these days.

Jack. His voice. His smile. His vivid blue eyes. His touch.

Memories of his lips on hers sent a thud of sensation straight through her. She set down the sandwich with a trembling hand, her minuscule appetite vanished in the face of her rampant fantasies.

Why didn't he ask to speak to her last night?

That thought returned unbidden as it had all during the sleepless night, for the whole of the morning. It had bubbled inside her, becoming a nagging ache that nothing could relieve. *Why didn't he want to talk to her?*

She could have asked to speak to him. She knew immediately it was him when he called. Mr. Willens had looked her way as he spoke to Jack, his silent question offering her the opportunity to ask for the phone next. But she'd shrugged, wanting a clear request from Jack to speak to her. A request that never came.

With a sigh, Rachel took a carrot curl from her plate and gazed around Mrs. Willens's homey country kitchen. A substantial maple dining table filled the space at one end, matching kitchen cabinetry at the other provided ample storage. The oak flooring glowed with care and the bright flowered curtains at the window were parted to let in a thick slice of noontime sun.

A collection of family photos were arrayed across the wall over the dining table. She smiled at the images of babies and toddlers, school pictures and graduation photos. Happy memories of a happy family.

One photo in particular caught her eye — two men standing side by side holding up a stringer of fish. Mr. Willens she recognized, although the shot had to be a good fifteen years old. The other man . . . his familiarity nagged at her. Heavens, if she didn't know better, she'd swear that other man was Mr. Hanford, Jack's father.

Mrs. Willens bustled in through the back door, distracting Rachel from the photos. "I'm getting myself some iced tea," Mrs. Willens said, tossing her gardening gloves on the counter. "Would you like some?"

"Yes, please," Rachel said, turning back to the pictures. "Who is this man with Mr. Willens? He looks amazingly like —"

Mrs. Willens snatched the photo in question from the wall and tucked it under her arm. "Is that old photo still out? He's just an old business associate of Georgie's."

"But he looks just like —"

The older woman shoved the photo into a drawer, then tsked at Rachel's full plate. "Is something wrong with your lunch?"

Rachel plucked the sandwich from her plate and took a huge bite. "No," she mumbled around the mouthful. "S'fine."

She chewed enthusiastically and swallowed. Mrs. Willens smiled, her eyes bright with humor. "Why don't you let me put the rest of that away until later when you're more hungry."

"But I'm hungry now," Rachel protested when Mrs. Willens whisked the plate from the table.

"No need to be polite," the woman said as she tore off a sheet of plastic wrap. "I've never been one to force food on a body." She tucked the wrap around the plate, then eyed Rachel shrewdly. "Any calls while I was outside?"

"Only one," Rachel told her, remembering how her heart had nearly exploded with hope when the phone rang. "A wrong number."

Mrs. Willens seemed almost as disappointed as Rachel had been. "Oh well," she said cryptically as she placed the sandwich in the refrigerator. She pulled out the pitcher of iced tea and poured herself a tall glass. "I'm headed out for another bout of weeding. I don't suppose you'd like to join me."

"Well . . ." Rachel said. Weeding was her least favorite springtime chore.

Mrs. Willens laughed. "I wasn't serious. I'm sure you'd rather take a nice nap or . . ." Her expression turned thoughtful. "I'll tell you what. I've got a bottle of some downright yummy bubble bath. Why don't you give some of that a try?"

What a temptation! At home, she never had more than ten uninterrupted minutes for anything as luxurious as a bubble bath. Her stepsisters always seemed to have one crisis or another that needed an immediate solution. Quick showers were the most she could squeeze into her busy life.

The thought of her sisters brought with it a wave of homesickness. She realized she hadn't spoken to Beulah or Bonnie since she'd left.

"I'd adore a bubble bath," Rachel told

Mrs. Willens and the older woman beamed. "But first, would you mind if I called my sisters? I have a calling card —"

"Don't you worry about that," Mrs. Willens admonished. "One little long distance call isn't going to break us. Go ahead and use the phone in your room."

Rachel gave her a grateful smile, then hurried off upstairs. She sighed with pleasure when she entered her room. They'd carried the country theme into the bedrooms as well, with frilly calico curtains and a braided rug on the hardwood floor. The high four-poster sat squarely in the center of the smallish room, the mattress covered with an intricate handmade quilt.

Rachel picked up her purse from the hope chest at the foot of the four-poster and rifled through it for her calling card. Despite Mrs. Willens's generous offer, Rachel felt more comfortable paying for the call herself.

She tapped out the access number on the bedside phone, then the digits of her home number. As the connection went through, she tried to remember her stepsisters' schedule. Was Bonnie still working at that diner? Was Beulah still attending her Spanish class? She hoped she'd catch at least one of her sisters at home.

Beulah answered on the fourth ring.

"Rachel!" she squealed with excitement. "Bonnie! It's Rachel!"

Rachel snatched the phone from her ear at Beulah's bellow, then cautiously brought it back. "How are you two doing?"

"Great! Marvelous! Bonnie, get on the extension!" she hollered, battering Rachel's ear again.

"Hi, Rachel," Bonnie chimed in, her voice mercifully softer than Beulah's. "We really miss you."

"I miss you guys, too," Rachel said. "Have I gotten many calls?"

"A bunch," Beulah told her. "I referred the business ones to Marilyn."

Marilyn was a top-notch seamstress Rachel had asked to fill in for her. "Thanks. Anything important in the mail I should know about?"

"A few bills," Bonnie said. "We'll take care of those."

"So how is he?" Beulah cut in.

"How is who?" Rachel hedged, although she knew who Beulah meant.

"That hunky Jack Hanford," Beulah said. "Is he a dynamite kisser?"

"Beulah!" Rachel scolded.

"Ah, c'mon Rachel, we know he was hot for you," Beulah persisted. "We just want the details."

"He must have kissed you by now," Bonnie said.

Rachel rubbed at her temple. She was a lousy liar and her sisters knew it. How was she going to answer?

"This really isn't any of your business," Rachel said, then could have bitten her tongue when she realized her words would only send up Beulah's radar scope.

"So he did kiss you," Beulah said gleefully. "How was it?"

Rachel supposed a little information wouldn't hurt. "Very nice."

Beulah pounced on the tremble in her voice. "Sounds like it was more than nice to me."

"Does he love you?" Bonnie asked eagerly.

"Don't be ridiculous," Rachel said.

"Do you love him?" Beulah asked.

All she had to say was no. She formed her lips to make the word, felt the sound of it in the back of her throat. A simple no, that's all she had to say.

If she hadn't been such a lousy liar.

The words came out as a bare whisper. "I think I do."

Horror washed over her at the realization. Her distress multiplied at the long, pin-drop silence at the other end of the line. Nothing, nothing could have quieted

209

her sisters except bone-deep shock.

"Oh," Beulah said finally, the word a soft puff of sound.

"Goodness," Bonnie added.

Rachel swallowed back her misery. "It's stupid," she said.

"It's not," Beulah insisted.

"It's wonderful," Bonnie put in.

Their vote of confidence only tightened the knot in Rachel's chest. "He doesn't love me."

"He must," Bonnie said. "He has to."

"He'd better," Beulah said, menace in her tone. Rachel took a tremulous breath. "I think he's attracted to me."

"You think?" Beulah asked.

"He's kissed me . . ." Rachel said, "a few times."

"Just kissed?" Bonnie asked.

"Well," Rachel said, feeling the heat rise in her cheeks, "a bit more than 'just.'" She sighed. "But I don't think I . . . light his rockets. I'm so plain."

She heard Beulah's exasperated snort. "You are *not* plain, Rachel Reeves. You just sometimes need . . ."

"A little perking up," Bonnie filled in.

"Maybe a little more decoration," Beulah added. A pause, then, "And we know just the thing."

"The one we saw yesterday?" Bonnie asked her sister.

"Red or black, what do you think?" Beulah asked Bonnie.

"Black, definitely," Bonnie said. "Much more classy."

"Can you pick it up after work?" Beulah asked.

"I think —"

"Excuse me," Rachel said, tired of being the pingpong ball in her sisters' conversation. "I really need to go."

"Where's your next stop?" Beulah asked. "There's something we want to send you."

Rachel dug in her purse for her copy of the itinerary. She read off the address of the hotel for Beulah.

"I love you both," Rachel said, surprised at how much she missed her exasperating sisters.

"We do, too," Bonnie said.

"We're so lucky to have you as a big sister, Rachel." Beulah said the words in a rush. "Bye."

Rachel stared, bemused, at the phone a moment after her sisters hung up. Then she set down the receiver and lay down on the bed. A bubble bath or a nap? she thought. What a positively decadent choice!

As the soft pillow cradled her head,

Rachel's eyelids grew heavy. A nap, and then a bubble bath. Why not treat herself with both?

She nudged off her sneakers, then hooked a toe under the neatly folded quilt at the foot of the bed. She pulled it up over her and snuggled under it with a sigh.

I love Jack.

Her eyes snapped open as the troubling thought intruded and stole the lassitude from her. What was she going to do? She couldn't very well declare herself, expose her vulnerable heart to him. He might not wish to hurt her, but his inability to return her love would wound her all the same.

She turned restlessly on the bed, willing her eyes shut. She would simply have to keep her feelings to herself. Then, when they said good-bye, she could do it with head held high, her pride still intact.

Although pride was cold consolation to the burning ache in her heart.

Jack hurried across the parking lot of the Mount Vernon airport, scanning the rows of cars for the red Camaro. His carry-on bag dug into his shoulder and his laden briefcase threatened to elongate his left arm. A quick look at his watch told him the bad news — it was nearly ten-thirty. That meant it would be well after midnight by the time he and Rachel got to their hotel.

The scrutiny of Hanford's financial reports had stretched long into the afternoon, until Jack despaired of catching a late afternoon flight out of Chicago. Then, when a four o'clock call to the airport confirmed that the next flight didn't leave until eight, his father dragged him off to dinner.

Henry's probing questions about Rachel during dinner raised a warning flag in Jack's brain, making him wonder all over again if Henry had his sights set on her as a future wife. But Moira, who had joined them for dinner, had just as many questions for him. Between their inquisition and his sharp yearning to be back with Rachel, his head spun by the time dinner was over.

Jack finally spotted his car and crossed to it with a sigh of relief. He quickly dumped his baggage into the trunk and climbed inside the car. The tension in his shoulders released when he at last pulled onto Interstate 64 toward Poseyville. The image of Rachel's face swam before his tired eyes, and he nudged the accelerator a little harder.

Another hour. He'd see her in another hour. He felt altogether too happy about that, he knew.

But he damn well didn't care.

Sixty-five minutes later, Jack pulled up to the Willenses' charming bed and breakfast with a sigh of relief. He climbed out of the car wearily, glad the hotel was only a fifteen minute drive away.

Mrs. Willens opened the door for him before he even had a chance to knock. She ushered him in with a broad smile. Mr. Willens rose from the sofa to shake his hand in welcome.

"Have a seat," Mrs. Willens offered. "I'll get you some coffee."

Jack shook his head. "I'd better not. We have to get to the hotel."

The Willenses exchanged a glance, then Mrs. Willens smiled up at him again. "But why go to a hotel? Why not just stay here for another night?"

Jack blinked, trying to order his tired mind. "Because," he said, scrambling for a plausible reason. "Because we can't."

"Of course you can," Mr. Willens said. "You can just head right on upstairs and climb in bed with your wife."

A crystal clear picture of himself doing just that seared through Jack's brain. He stood dumbfounded a moment, rooted by the power of that image. Then he shook his head, trying to dislodge the notion.

"We have to go to the hotel," he said. They did, didn't they?

"But Rachel is already asleep," Mrs. Willens said. "Even with an afternoon nap, she barely made it through dinner."

"You've been working that young lady far too hard," Mr. Willens chastised.

"She's asleep?" Jack parroted. "Rachel's asleep?" He sounded like an idiot, but his tiredness coupled with the keen draw of seeing Rachel again stole his intelligence.

Mrs. Willens hooked her arm in his. "I'll just take you on upstairs to your room. Georgie, you go get Jack's bag from the car and bring it up."

"Right-o," Mr. Willens said. "I'll just take those keys . . ."

Mr. Willens pulled the car keys from Jack's nerveless fingers as Mrs. Willens escorted him up the curving stairs. Alarm, excitement and anticipation battled it out inside him as they reached the upstairs landing.

"Here we are," Mrs. Willens said softly as she stopped before the first door off the landing. She put a finger to her lips. "Remember, she's asleep."

As Mrs. Willens returned downstairs, Jack nudged open the door. The faint glow of a nightlight illuminated the room just enough for him to make out Rachel's slender form on the bed. He felt a pressure in his chest as he gazed at her, the gold silk of her hair spread across the pillow, the curve of her cheek, her slightly parted lips.

He'd taken a step toward her when he heard footsteps on the stairs. He poked his head out to see Mr. Willens step up to the landing with his carry-on bag.

"I left the briefcase," Mr. Willens whispered.

Jack nodded his thanks as he took the carry-on. Then he ducked back into the room and softly shut the door.

The slight noise was enough to wake Rachel. Her eyes fluttered open and her gaze fixed on him.

"Hello," she said, her voice liquid with sleep. "You made it."

"Yes." He moved closer to the bed, drawn by a gentle scent that drifted from her. It reminded him of honeysuckle.

"I guess I should get up and get dressed," she said. "So we can go to the hotel."

Jack drew in a lungful of fragrance. "We're not going. We're staying here tonight."

That woke her. She eyed him warily. "But where will you sleep?"

"Here," he said, not bothering to suppress a smile. "With my wife."

"Here?" Her tongue slipped out to wet

her lips and heat pooled in his groin. "But where?"

Beside you, he wanted to say. With you in my arms.

He pulled his gaze from her, scanned the room. "I suppose I could push those two chairs together."

Rachel glanced at the two occasional chairs set on either side of a small table. "You can't possibly fit there. I can sleep in the chairs, you take the bed."

She threw off the blankets and another cloud of scent curled around him. When she would have climbed from the bed, he put out a hand to stop her.

And found his palm curved around her bare shoulder. His gaze fell to her satiny gown, to the hem that had slid up just above her knees.

Rachel yanked down the ivory gown, covering herself again. "Mrs. Willens suggested I change for bed since you were getting in so late. I'd intended to put on something decent when you arrived."

"But you fell asleep," he said, unable to resist running a finger under the narrow shoulder strap of the gown. A question nagged at him, distracting him from her soft, fragrant skin. "Mrs. Willens told you to dress for bed?"

She gazed up at him, her hazel eyes dark in the dim light. "Yes. Since I was so tired. That way I could sleep more comfortably."

Something seemed awry in Rachel's explanation, something to do with Mr. and Mrs. Willens. But the warming of Rachel's skin under his palm drew him in more pleasurable directions and he let the matter go.

He skimmed his palm down her bare arm, then linked his fingers with hers. "We could both sleep in the bed," he murmured.

Her eyes widened. He saw the motion of her throat as she swallowed. "We could?"

"Just sleep," he assured her. "Me on my side, you on yours."

She nodded cautiously. "I suppose that would be okay. I would hate for you to be scrunched in those chairs."

He released her fingers and skidded his hand up her arm again. "I don't have pajamas, but I have a pair of sweats I can wear. For modesty's sake."

Her eyes fluttered shut when his fingers grazed her throat. He realized how insane an idea it was to consider sharing Rachel's bed. But he could no more turn down the opportunity than he could stop breathing.

He could at least be a gentleman about it. "I promise I won't touch you."

That he was already touching her apparently wasn't lost on Rachel. She gave him a wry glance. Then her mouth curved into a gentle smile. "Okay. We can try it."

He stepped back from her and turned to find the suitcases he'd left behind with her that held the rest of his clothes. He found his sweatpants in the larger of the two, then pulled his toiletries from his carry-on.

By the time he'd finished in the bathroom, she'd already climbed back into bed. She lay on her back, squarely on her own side of the bed, blanket pulled up to her chin.

Jack rounded the bed to the opposite side and folded back the blankets. The sheets smelled of her and when he gingerly laid his head on the pillow, her scent lingered there as well. He held himself stiffly beside her, jaw set, every part of his anatomy screamingly aware of her only inches away.

Several minutes later, he realized the fallacy of lying in bed beside her. He'd never be able to sleep with her so near. He would have done as well to sleep in the chairs for all the rest he was likely to get tonight.

Then he felt her tentative touch against his hand and in another moment, her fingers were nestled against his palm. That bare contact started a wildfire of sensation and emotion within him. He felt a familiar heaviness in his loins as his willing mind laid out one erotic fantasy after another, each one starring him and Rachel.

But something else threaded through the fantasies, a surge of protectiveness, of possessiveness. He wanted nothing more than to hold her, to keep her forever by his side. Those emotions filled him with stark terror, filled him with joy.

Despite the clamoring in his mind, the tightness in his body, he turned and tugged Rachel closer. He spooned her against him, urging her head against his shoulder, her hips in the cradle of his. Gritting his teeth against the feel of her softness pressing against his hard length, he forced his eyes to close.

Rachel lay tense for a moment, then the warmth and the darkness must have overcome her. Her body relaxed, her breathing steadied, and her head grew heavy on his arm. While his heart celebrated that sweet weight, his own tiredness took its toll. Despite his certainty that he could never sleep with her in his arms, Jack drifted into a welcome oblivion.

Chapter 10

Rachel woke slowly, bathed in a delicious sense of well-being. Her cheek rested against Jack's firm biceps, and his heat warmed the whole of her side. His body curved toward her, so that his free arm lay loosely across her waist. His bent knee rested on her thigh.

She kept her eyes closed to prolong the moment. How would it feel to wake up every day with Jack beside her, holding her in his arms? Even her wildest fantasies couldn't match this bliss.

She sighed and reminded herself that this wasn't real. They'd been forced together by the situation, that was all. It didn't mean that Jack would wake and turn to her and profess his undying love. That only happened in fiction.

Tightness in her chest replaced her sweet contentment. She had to get up, away from the seductive pleasure of Jack's arms, away from the hopeless dreams his touch created. She had enough heartache on the horizon, when she and Jack parted company at the end of her employment with him. She didn't need to compound her pain with useless wishes.

She shifted, lifting her head from Jack's arm, and tried to pull free of his weight. But his hand gripped her waist and his leg snugged more firmly over hers. She flicked a sideways glance at him, taking in his closed eyes, the faint roughness of morning beard on his cheeks. He must be still asleep, unaware that he was holding her so tightly.

Rachel tried again, pulling away more firmly. This time his fingers splayed across her waist, implacably holding her in place. She felt his breath on her cheek.

"Stay put," he growled in her ear, sounding only half awake.

The low, sexy sound of his voice sent a shiver along the length of her. Ruthlessly, she quashed it.

"I need to get up," she said primly.

He pressed more firmly against her. "Don't want you to," he said sleepily.

Jack tucked her closely to him, and she felt his unmistakable hardness against her hip. Sensation lanced through her again, this time shooting straight to her core, stealing her breath away.

She never would have thought a man's arousal would feel so glorious. Shocking impulses coursed through her. All at once, she wanted to rub against him, to circle his length with her fingers, to wrap her legs around him and press her center against his rock-hard flesh.

Rachel couldn't help herself — she moved against him, curving her hip closer, her body bending toward him like a flower toward the sun. The greater pressure drove a gasp from her lungs, then quickened her breathing.

"Lord, Rachel." His whole body went rigid and she sensed he was now thoroughly awake. "If you don't stop now, you'll be getting a hell of a lot more than you bargained for."

His words threw a cold splash of mortification over her and she jerked free of his arms. She scrambled off the bed, then stood looking over him, arms crossed over her breasts.

"You're the one who wouldn't let me go," she said, chin lifted.

Jack grinned at her, unrepentant. "I wasn't awake yet. You took advantage of me." He yawned, then reached for his watch on the bedside table. "We'd better get going.

We're expected at a pancake breakfast this morning."

She stood there another moment, shivering, then with a nod, turned on her heel and headed for the bathroom. She was about to close the door when she realized she needed a change of clothes. With an exasperated sigh, she stomped back into the bedroom.

And immediately halted her in her tracks. There stood Jack beside the bed, the front of his black sweatpants jutting out with his unmistakable arousal.

Rachel couldn't look away. All she could think of was his hard length pressed against her, the wild impulses that had rampaged through her brain. And despite the lazy smile she sensed on his face, her lascivious side just had to look its fill.

Finally, she dragged her gaze away, heat rising in her cheeks. Ignoring his grin, she grabbed up her nearest suitcase and hauled it into the bathroom. With what dignity she could, she kept her eyes averted from his tempting body until the bathroom door closed.

Setting down the suitcase, Rachel raised her trembling hands to her cheeks to cool them. She stared at herself in the bathroom mirror, shocked at the brightness of her eyes, at the fullness of her lips. He hadn't even kissed her, yet she felt as aroused as if he had.

Her gaze fell on the sink and the items arranged there. His toothbrush and toothpaste lay cozied up next to hers, his razor on top of her hairbrush. Somehow the co-mingling of their personal things seemed nearly as intimate as the night they had shared together.

Turning on the faucet, she dashed cupped handfuls of cold water over her face. A shred of her sanity restored, she ran through her morning routine quickly, mindful of Jack waiting for her on the other side of the door. After a rapid survey of her suitcase, she pulled out a silky shirt of coral and pale turquoise and a pair of coral slacks. After dressing, she plucked her toiletries from beside Jack's, then stuffed them and her gown into her suitcase.

She grabbed her suitcase, then reached for the door. She hesitated. What if Jack lost patience, and decided to change in the bedroom? What if she were to open the door and caught him in the buff, his glorious body in full view?

Wouldn't that be awful? she thought with a grin. She was still smiling when she did open the door and found Jack, bare-chested in his black sweats, leaning against the foot of the bed.

He eyed her grin with suspicion. "What?"

She just shook her head. A considering smile spread across his face. He gathered up a pile of clothes from the bed and moved past her into the bathroom. Before he shut the door, he leaned out and brushed a kiss on her cheek.

Rachel pressed a hand against her cheek as if to hold the sensation there. Then, with a sigh, she moved through the room, making a last minute check for belongings. By the time Jack reappeared in a pale blue shirt and navy slacks, she was ready to go downstairs.

As Jack pulled onto the interstate, Rachel thought wistfully of the beautiful breakfast the Willenses had laid out on the dining room table. The two guests that had arrived the night before had just begun digging into plates piled high with orange French toast and apple sausage when Rachel and Jack had said their good-byes.

"I suppose I should be grateful for the scones," Rachel said, gazing down at the two napkin-wrapped pastries in her lap.

Jack kept his gaze on the other cars as he merged into the I-64 traffic. "You know, you'll have to feed me."

"Feed you?"

"You wouldn't want me to try to drive and eat at the same time. That could be hazardous."

She didn't doubt that he could manage the task quite safely. Not wanting to give in so easily, she gave him an impish grin, "You could wait until we get to the pancake breakfast."

He shook his head. "How would that look, Mr. and Mrs. Hanford, eating scones at a Hanford pancake breakfast?"

She pretended to give that considerable thought, but the image of placing warm bites of the flaky pastry into his mouth kept intruding. "I suppose you're right," she conceded, then broke off a morsel of scone.

The first bite he took quite properly, catching the pastry with his teeth and bringing it into his mouth. The next bite, his sharp white teeth nipped closer to her fingers and his lips brushed against her finger tips before she could pull away. The third piece, his tongue moved past the warm scone to taste her, the tip flicking against her skin. Startled by the quick rush of sensation, she dropped the scone in his lap.

She reached for it in reaction before she realized the foolhardiness of her action. When his thighs closed, trapping her hand, she realized her error. Her face flushed at her boldness, but she didn't pull her hand free immediately. She took her time, sliding her palm along the smooth fabric of his slacks, her thumb achingly close to the hard ridge she could see growing at his fly.

The rattle of speed bumps on the interstate shook her back to attention. Jack released her hand and brushed the crumbs of the scone to the floor of the car.

"I suppose I'd better pay more attention to my driving," he said wryly.

Rachel picked up the other scone and nibbled at it, her appetite stolen by the tension in her stomach. She thought she should have felt more ashamed by her actions, but all she could think of was another opportunity to touch him.

A minute later, the familiar mauve and pale rose Hanford House of Pancakes sign appeared beside the interstate. Jack pulled off and made his way to the restaurant parking lot. He parked at the far end of the crowded lot and they climbed out of the car.

"This is a fund-raiser for one of the local middle schools," Jack told her as they wended their way through the tables and benches that had been set up at one end of the lot. "Hanford's is providing the equipment and supplies, the students are providing the labor."

They made their way to the propane griddles set up beyond the tables. Bubbling pancakes and sizzling sausage filled the griddle. Several white-aproned boys and girls in their early teens flipped pancakes while others delivered breakfasts to the patrons at the tables.

"What a marvelous idea," Rachel said as they watched the excited young men and women work.

"It is," Jack agreed. "A lot of people say this sort of thing is good public relations, which it is. But I like doing it because it's just plain fun."

"So what do we do?" Rachel asked, watching one of the students expertly flip a pancake.

"Their teacher's the one who organized this. We'll ask him."

They approached a tall, bony young man with his dark hair drawn back into a ponytail. He wore a plastic apron over his clothes and was just breaking open another box of sausage.

"Mr. Hanford! It's so great to see you," the teacher said.

Jack nudged her forward. "Mike Clark, I'd like you to meet Rachel Hanford." Jack winked at her. "The missus."

She shook Mike's hand, then gestured around at the busy students. "They're doing such a great job."

"Thanks to this man right here," Mike said, patting Jack's arm. "This group of kids don't get many breaks. They're the ones that don't fit in, that can't make it in a regular classroom. This is an incredible opportunity Jack's giving them."

"I'm just glad they'll have a chance to go on that end-of-year camping trip," Jack said. "So what do you want us to do?"

Mike gazed around at his students. "Jaime and Felicia could use a break at the grill." He grinned at Jack. "I suppose you know a little bit about making pancakes."

Jack laughed. "I was cooking flapjacks before I could walk. Lead me to 'em."

Mike found aprons for Jack and Rachel, then they relieved the two students of their spatulas. After a quick refill of pancake batter from the restaurant's kitchen, they were ready to cook.

"Pancakes or sausages?" Jack asked.

Rachel eyed the full box of links beside the griddle. "I'll start with sausages, then maybe you can promote me to pancakes."

As Rachel pulled handfuls of cold sausage from the box, Jack picked up the pitcher of batter. With an expert flick of the wrist, he poured out the exact amount of batter for a perfectly sized pancake.

Rachel watched in admiration as he served out batter for seven more just like the first. "I can see this will take some practice on my part."

"It's more than practice," Jack said as he checked the underside of the first pancake. "It is understanding the soul of the pancake, its inner self."

He turned to her, his expression serious, then he grinned. Rachel burst out laughing, then, still chuckling, returned her attention to her sausages. She rolled each one with her spatula so that they'd brown evenly.

"I'm glad sausage cooking isn't quite as much a philosophical challenge. That was one class I barely passed in college."

Jack quickly turned his pancakes, one after another, each one a delectable golden hue. Once the other side cooked as well, he served them up, two to a plate. Rachel added sausages to each. After placing a wedge of orange on the side, the students carried the plates out to the tables.

For nearly an hour, Jack and Rachel worked companionably side by side, cooking and serving up pancakes and sausage. When the crowd began to thin and there was only a handful waiting to eat, Rachel decided it was time to switch places.

"Now's the time to teach me the magic of pancake preparation," she told Jack, "when there are fewer people left to starve while I fumble through it."

"You talk as if you've never made pancakes."

"I've only made ordinary flapjacks," she told him with an expansive gesture. "Never Zen pancakes."

He stepped back and invited her to his side of the griddle. She expected him to trade places with her, but instead, he moved to stand behind her. When she reached for the pitcher of batter, he placed his hand over hers.

"Jaime," Jack said, interrupting the slight young man from his flirting with a pretty classmate. "Would you watch the sausages, please?"

"Sure thing, man," Jaime said, returning to the griddle. Jack urged Rachel to pick up the pitcher, then together they held it suspended above the griddle. "It's all in the wrist," Jack said, his mouth close to her ear. "You have to have just the right amount of bend."

With that, they tipped the pitcher and batter flowed out onto the griddle. Rachel knew she should watch how much batter was spilling out, but the feel of Jack's arm along hers proved too much distraction. The puddle of batter grew and grew until Jack finally jerked the pitcher back.

"I can see you need a great deal of practice," Jack said, moving in even closer. He nudged her hand again, and this time they produced a normal-sized pancake.

"This would be easier if you weren't so close to me," she said, snuggling back against him.

"Easier, but not nearly as much fun."

The batter poured, they set down the pitcher. Rachel eyed her mistake, nearly the size of a dinner plate. "How in the world will we turn that big one?"

"Cooperation," he murmured in her ear.

While they waited for the pancakes to cook, Jack put his arms around her waist, his chest nestled against her back. Rachel felt a little like one of those puddles of pancake batter — limp and nerveless and getting hotter by the second.

"Time to turn," Jack said, picking up the spatula. He handed it to her, then curled his fingers around hers.

They started with the normal-sized ones, slipping the spatula underneath and quickly flipping each one. Rachel only messed two up, accidentally flopping one half onto another so that they were joined. Jack swiftly repaired her mistake.

"Now, Big Daddy," he said, guiding her to the mammoth flapjack. "First we loosen it." They ran the spatula under it, all around its edges. "Ready? One, two . . ."

On three, they turned the big pancake. It broke slightly and landed on top of a sausage, but other than that, it was perfect.

"That one's ours," Rachel said as she turned back to the other pancakes. She was proud of how neatly she stacked them onto their plates, how the touch of Jack's palm on the back of her hand barely distracted her. She even managed to hoist Big Daddy onto a plate intact.

"I think Jaime and Felicia can finish up here," Jack said, tugging the spatula from Rachel's hand and giving it to the boy.

They took their plate to a table and Rachel seated herself. Jack sat next to her, straddling the bench.

When Rachel reached for her fork, Jack took it from her. "My turn," he said, cutting a wedge of pancake. He poured a puddle of syrup onto the plate and dipped the bite into it.

After her experience at the commercial shoot, Rachel never would have thought she'd want to eat pancakes again. But when Jack's hand held the fork, she supposed she would even eat Brussels sprouts, the most dreaded of vegetables.

She opened her mouth, then closed her lips on the bite of pancake when Jack offered it. He slipped the fork out, then grazed the tines gently across her lower lip.

Lord, who would have thought pancake eating would be so erotic? Of course, everything with Jack was erotic, from skating to pancake cooking. She could live her life quite happily finding all the sexy little things she could do with Jack.

Jack served her half the pancake, each bite making her hotter than the last, then offered her the fork. She fed him, her gaze locked on his, his blue eyes nearly igniting her as he licked sweet syrup from his lips.

"We'd better go," he said at last, his voice ragged.

"You haven't finished your pancake," she said.

He leaned close so that only she could hear. "Right now, the only thing I want to eat is you."

Nervous excitement skittered up her spine. Rachel pressed her cheek against his, nuzzling against him, but Jack pulled away from her. "I shouldn't have said that," he said, rising from the bench.

"What's wrong?" Rachel asked, confused.

He took her arm. "Let's say our good-byes." They found Mike, again accepted his thanks, then headed back to their car.

"Where are we going?" Rachel asked.

"To our next stop," Jack said tightly. "We have a dinner to attend tonight."

Rachel wondered at his sudden change of mood. "Are you angry about something?"

"No." The clipped word said otherwise. "I just want to get to the hotel so that we have enough time to relax before dinner."

Rachel subsided into silence, her stomach clenching. She couldn't help wondering if he'd begun to feel embarrassed by their erotic by-play. Maybe he'd realized how foolish it was to lead her on, to give her hope when he knew he had no desire for a real relationship with her.

Sunk in her misery, Rachel stared blindly at the passing scenery. When they reached the Elberfeld exit, she felt relief that soon they would be at the hotel and she could escape his presence.

She waited in the hotel lobby while Jack checked them in. To her surprise, when he returned to her, he had a package in his hand.

"Looks like you got something from your

sisters," he said, handing her the white FedEx envelope.

She took the package and hefted its slight weight. "I can't imagine . . ." Her voice trailed off as she remembered her conversation with them yesterday. She almost dreaded seeing what was inside.

"Let's go on up," Jack said, motioning her to the elevators. "We've got adjoining rooms this time. They didn't have a suite."

The rooms were much less luxurious than what they'd been used to, but clean and neat. Rachel tossed her purse on the bed with a sigh, then placed the envelope from her sisters on the dresser. The package might not hold dynamite, but she had a feeling it would be just as explosive.

She opened the door to the bellman's knock, then stepped aside while he carried in her suitcases. After tipping him, she opened the adjoining door.

Jack had opened his as well. She peeked inside at the mirror image to her room. Jack had stretched out on the bed and was speaking on the phone.

He waved at her, but didn't invite her inside. Turning away, Rachel decided to bite the bullet and see what her sisters had sent her. If nothing else, the contents would probably cheer her up.

She tugged the adhesive flap open. She wondered if she ought to peek inside first to prepare herself. Then she figured she could use the shock value of her sisters' gift and she dumped it out onto the dresser top.

A wad of flaming red tissue paper slipped from the envelope. A satiny black strap dangled from the tissue, giving her a warning of what lay inside. As cautious as if the wrappings held a snake, Rachel pulled aside the fragile red paper.

It took her a moment to comprehend the bit of black satin, tiny red ribbons and scarlet lace edging. She picked it up and held it out, trying to figure out what she was looking at. Then she realized she had it upside down.

Turning it so that the garter straps hung properly, she gazed, bemused, at her sisters' gift. The sexy black frippery was a merry widow, in fact, one of her own design. It wasn't one that she'd made herself — a quick check of the manufacturer's tag confirmed it — but this was one of the first designs she'd sold.

Still nested in the red tissue were a pair of lacy black undies and silky black stockings. She fingered the deliciously slippery stuff, wondering how they would feel against her legs.

It touched her that her sisters had bought her such beautiful things, although she could never possibly wear them. She'd designed the merry widow for racy, sexy women, certainly not someone like herself. She couldn't begin to imagine herself in it.

Or could she?

She glanced quickly at the adjoining door. She could still hear the low rumble of Jack's voice in the other room. Just the sound of it went straight through her, tickling her nerve endings. Somehow, that heightened awareness made her feel just as sexy and daring as the women for whom she'd designed the merry widow.

She *could* just try it on. She didn't have to show anyone, most especially not Jack. She could go into the bathroom, slip it on, look at herself in the mirror, then take it off again. Jack would never be the wiser.

Holding the pile of satin and lace close to her chest, she crept past the open adjoining door into the bathroom. Once safely behind the locked bathroom door, she set the merry widow, panties and stockings on the counter and quickly shucked her blouse and slacks. She dithered over her bra, then decided she'd have to take it off for the full effect.

She quickly slipped on the panties, then picked up the merry widow and held it out.

The strapless black garment nipped in at the waist like an hour glass. Thin red satin ribbon crisscrossed the front in a mock closure. There was a zipper in the back that went the length of the garment, making it a snap to put on. A frilly red tassel hung from the zipper tab to make it easy to reach the zipper.

Quickly, before she lost her nerve, Rachel unzipped the merry widow. She stepped into it, then pulled it up over her hips. Reaching back behind her, she fumbled for the zipper in the back. Her finger tips brushed against the slippery tassel a few times before she could get hold of it.

Sucking in her stomach, she tugged at the tassel. Halfway up, she had to switch hands, reaching over her shoulder to close the zipper the rest of the way. A few of the tassel strands caught in the zipper teeth before it was quite to the top, but the merry widow was so snug, it didn't matter that the closure gapped an inch.

It took some doing to bend over in the stiff garment to tug on the stockings, but she managed. After clipping the garters into the top of the stockings, she smoothed the merry widow down over her hips and peeked into the mirror.

Her breath caught at her first glimpse of herself. Her creamy breasts filled the front of the merry widow, nearly spilling from the top. Her waist seemed impossibly narrow, her hips flared to a womanly roundness. Her lacy black panties made a provocative vee at the juncture of her legs. The contrast between the ivory of her thighs and the black of her stockings was downright decadent.

Oh, if only she had the nerve to let Jack see her like this. If only she could walk boldly out of this room and into Jack's arms. Closing her eyes, she pictured his reaction to her sashaying through the connecting doors and across his room toward him. She imagined his surprise, his shock, then those emotions fading into hot passion.

She allowed herself a few more moments of delicious fantasy, then opened her eyes again. Gazing at her reflection, she let out a long, tremulous sigh. Why dream of something she couldn't possibly do? Why dream of rousing Jack's passion when what she really wanted was something entirely different?

His love.

Something squeezed tight in her chest and she felt the prick of tears. It seemed that since she'd admitted to her sisters that she loved Jack, a dam had crumbled, letting loose a flood of emotions she couldn't control. Her love for him burned in her heart, growing stronger with each day, each moment.

Angrily swiping the tears from her cheeks, she decided she'd had enough of her playacting. Wriggling her arm back behind her, she searched for the tassel with her finger tips. She snagged a few strands with her fingers and pulled.

Nothing happened. She pulled harder. The tassel gave way to her tugging and she waited for the ease of the opening zipper. But her tugging didn't open the zipper, it pulled free the three strands of tassel she was clinging to.

Rachel stared dumbly down at the shiny red strings in her hand. Why would the tassel be falling apart? She turned her back to the mirror, then craned her neck over her shoulder to look. To her horror, she saw that the strands of the tassel had become hopelessly entangled in the zipper. Now not only was the tassel falling apart, the zipper was jammed.

Snaking her left arm up her back, she groped for the zipper tab. But try as she might, she couldn't quite reach the top of the zipper. She changed tactics, reaching down over her shoulder with her right arm. She could just brush the small tab, but there was no way she would have enough leverage to tug it free of the tangle.

Straining even harder with her left arm, she contorted it painfully up her back, pushing herself inch by inch up her spine. When she reached the tassel, she grabbed a handful. Gripping it tightly, she wrenched it down. The stiff garment folded down an inch, but the zipper refused to give.

Rachel was trapped in this silly thing, a prisoner to satin and lace. Her mouth twitched upward at the sheer ludicrousness of the situation and she entertained a brief fantasy of living the rest of her life encased in a black merry widow.

A rap on the door startled her out of her reverie. "Rachel?" Jack called out through the door. "Are you okay?"

"F-fine," Rachel stuttered. "I'm fine."

A moment of silence outside the door, then Jack said, "There's something I want to talk to you about."

"Now?" she squeaked. She cleared her throat and tried again. "You want to talk now?"

"Are you in the tub?"

"No. I mean yes. I mean I can't —"

"Rachel, what's going on?"

"Ah," she stalled. "I'm doing my nails."

"Then you won't mind me coming in."

"Well, I . . ." Rachel temporized.

What now? Should she throw on her clothes over the merry widow and open the door? She scrutinized her blouse and slacks lying rumpled on the floor. Their fabric was so lightweight, the merry widow would show right through.

The door rattled as Jack tried the lock. "Rachel, if you don't come out, I'm coming in."

She chewed on her lower lip, a mass of indecision. Then she spied the white hotel towels hanging on their rack.

"Just a minute!" Moving quickly, she snatched up a towel and whipped it around her. Then she reached over to unlock the door and stepped back to allow Jack to let himself in.

His eyes raked her body, as if he were assuring himself she was alright. Then his gaze returned to her legs and Rachel realized her fatal error. She'd forgotten about the hose.

"What in the world are you wearing?" he asked, his eyes riveted on her legs.

Rachel tried to pull the corner of the towel down to cover her thighs, but that only exposed the top of the merry widow. "Nothing . . . I mean . . ."

In the face of the bright interest in his eyes, Rachel squeezed her own shut and took a long, deep breath. Then she met

Jack's gaze and with slow, deliberate movements, she unwrapped the towel.

"It's called a merry widow," she told him, dropping the towel on the floor.

She'd never seen a man look so stunned. If she'd whacked him on the side of the head with a two-by-four right now, he probably wouldn't even notice.

"It's . . . it's . . ." he gasped.

"Beulah and Bonnie sent it to me," she said. "My sisters. That's what was in that package. I think they wanted to send me something to cheer me up, so they went out and bought it for me. It was very sweet really, especially since it's one of my own designs, except —"

"You designed this?" he broke into her babbling.

She nodded. He took a step toward her. "It looks . . . snug," he managed.

"It is a bit. A little hard to breathe."

Then he ran a finger tip along the satin at her waist, and breathing became impossible. He fingered the red ribbons in the front. "Is this how you take it off?" he asked hoarsely.

She shook her head. "There's a zipper in the back." She dragged in a difficult breath, swallowed hard.

"And it's stuck."

Chapter 11

Jack's hands trembled as he absorbed what she'd said. "The zipper's stuck?"

Her wide hazel eyes seemed luminescent as she gazed up at him. "Yes," she said softly. "It's caught on the tassel."

"Do you need help?" He'd tried to say the words in a very matter-of-fact way, but they sounded like seduction. He swallowed against a dry throat and tried again. "I could get it unstuck for you."

She nodded, then turned slowly to present her back. He'd thought her creamy breasts would be hidden from him in this position, but with his greater height, he had a very nice view of the soft mounds and the shadowy cleft between them. Not to mention the narrow expanse of her bare shoulders.

He forced his focus to the jammed zipper. Indeed, several strands of a silky red tassel had lodged in the teeth and it would take some patient picking to pull them free. He might even manage to do it without touching her skin. The most difficult part would be ignoring his fantasies of stripping off the lace panties and taking her — up on the counter, against the wall — without ever removing the merry widow.

He kicked himself mentally for even entertaining the thought. Hadn't he just spent the last hour lecturing himself on how wrong it was to lead Rachel on? To touch her, to tease her, when he would never be able to offer her a relationship beyond the physical? As hot as that physical coming together would be, he wanted no part of marriage, no part of commitment. And he knew commitment was exactly what Rachel wanted, what she deserved.

"Well?" Rachel asked, interrupting his thoughts. "Can you do it?"

No. I can't, he thought. *I can't love you.* As much as he might have wanted to believe that what he felt for Rachel was love, he knew he was only fooling himself. Love was just lust that burst into flower, then withered just as quickly.

"Yes, I think so," he answered.

Setting his jaw, he studied the zipper again. He'd try to pull the strands free, one by one, then see if that was enough to release the zipper.

Once all the tassel strands were free, he tugged at the zipper tab. It wouldn't budge. The top of the merry widow would give with each tug while the zipper stayed put. He realized he would have to hold the top of the garment while he pulled down the zipper.

Cautiously, he slipped his fingers inside the merry widow. The warmth of Rachel's soft flesh immediately seeped into his fingers, distracting him from what he was supposed to do. For a moment, he stroked her with the back of his fingers, drawing one finger along the indentation of her spine.

"How's it going?" she whispered, drawing him back to his task.

"Fine," he muttered, then gripped the top of the red-edged black satin. The zipper still resisted, so that he had to readjust for a better grip, which brought more of his hand in contact with Rachel's skin. Occasionally silky strands of her hair would brush against his arm, adding to the sensual assault.

With a determination borne of desperation, Jack yanked hard at the zipper and it finally gave way, opening to the bottom of the merry widow. Jack stared at the pale vee, and of their own accord, his hands slipped inside.

Parting the zipper, he stroked along her back, his thumbs gliding down the indentation of her spine. When he reached her tiny waist, he circled it with his hands. The loosened merry widow slipped down, exposing Rachel's breasts.

"Jack?"

Rachel's soft, liquid voice wrapped around him. "Tell me to stop, Rachel," he rasped out, his hands easing up to just below her breasts.

Her answer was a bare thread of sound. "I don't want you to stop."

His response was half growl, half cry of possession as he turned her and pressed her against him. Rachel thought she would explode with the first touch of his lips against hers, that she would burst into flame. He pulled her so tightly against him she had to struggle to breathe, yet she wanted to be closer still.

He buried one hand in her hair, the other lay against the bare skin of her back. To be nearly nude while he was fully dressed was impossibly erotic. A shocking series of images raced through her mind — of her pushing him to the floor, stripping off her panties and loosing him from his slacks.

Her lascivious impulses frightened her.

She was terrified that she might do something stupid and awkward and ruin everything.

Rachel pulled back from his kiss, gasping for breath. "Jack," she panted, "I've never . . ."

She left the thought unfinished, grateful when he understood, scared that that might be enough to make him change his mind. But he drew a finger tip down her cheek. "Then we'll have to go more slowly," he said.

Stepping back from her, Jack lifted her in his arms. Holding her close to him, he strode into her room and set her on the edge of the bed. Stripping back the covers, he guided her down to the pillow.

He stroked her body through the merry widow. "This is so incredibly sexy. I thought my heart would stop when I first saw you in it."

"Sexy, maybe, but not terribly comfortable," she said, trying to shift so that the zipper didn't dig into her back.

"We'd better take care of that," he said, and his fingers drifted down to the garters.

He studied the garter clips a moment, then with a flick of his thumb, released the first one. He moved to her other leg, and opened the front garter there as well.

"Turn over," he said, his hands on her body urging her to do so. Her breath caught as his hands stroked underneath the garter strap, heating the tender flesh of her upper thighs.

Jack released the last two garters, then returned her to her back. "Lift up," he said. She did and he tugged down the merry widow, his gaze burning every exposed inch of her body. Once it was free of her hips, he pulled the garment down her legs, then tossed it aside. He stood over her a long moment, his gaze raking her, as palpable as a touch.

"This isn't fair," she protested.

His finger tips scudded along her belly, sending shivers through her. "What?" he asked as he continued his lazy exploration.

"I want to see you, too," she said, forcing the words past her embarrassment. She gulped. "All of you."

He grinned and her heart slammed into overdrive. Then his fingers moved to the buttons of his shirt and he quickly slipped them free. He threw off his shirt, then stepped out of his slacks.

Rachel had to struggle to breathe as she explored him with her gaze. She'd seen his muscled chest before, the soft furring of golden hair covering it. But his powerful legs were a revelation, more hair-roughened than his chest, their muscled length begging her to run her hands down them. She imagined the feel of them, the coarse hair against her palms, the heated skin burning her.

Then she brought her gaze to his navy briefs. His jutting manhood fascinated her as much as it had that morning. A shocking urge coursed through her, to rest her cheek against it, to rub along its length.

"Seen enough?" he asked, his mouth curved into a faint smile.

She smiled coquettishly in return. "For now."

He leaned over her, urging her to scoot over. Then he stretched out beside her and turned her toward him.

"We'll take this as fast, or as slow as you want," he said, his expression serious. "I'll stop anytime you want."

She drew a hand down his cheek, loving the rough feel of it. "I won't want to stop."

His gaze locked with hers, he moved his hand slowly down her body. Tugging on her thigh, he brought it up over his hip. He toyed with the silky black hose.

"I like these," he said, fingers dipping inside.

Rachel shuddered in reaction. "Should I take them off?"

"Leave them," he said. He slid his hand up to her derriere and cupped it, pulling her close to him.

"Rachel," he murmured, then his mouth closed on hers.

He sipped at her mouth, tiny kisses that feathered along her lips, across her jaw. He teased her with the tip of his tongue, leaving a moist, hot trail.

She wanted to touch him all over. She moved her hand tentatively along his side, over the firm musculature of his back. Each time she dipped close to the waistband of his briefs, she retreated, frightened by the compulsion to explore there.

Jack moved his hand up, past her lacy panties, to her waist, along her side. Higher, until he skimmed the side of her breast with his thumb, drawing a gasp from her.

Her nipples beaded, hard and sensitive, begging for his touch. She thought she would die waiting for his hand to move again. When he did, his thumb grazed the sensitive peak, her hips bucked against him, a response she was helpless to control.

His thumb brushed her nipple again, then he covered her breast with his large hand and skimmed his palm against it in a circular motion. Her nipple rubbed along his palm, the sensation building, drawing a taut wire of connection between her breast and the center of her.

Rachel pressed against him more tightly, his hardness at the juncture of her legs, the friction of his body exciting her beyond belief. She pushed her leg higher on his hip, positioning the now-damp center of her firmly against him.

Jack plunged his tongue into her mouth and with each thrust, drove his hips toward her in matching rhythm. Rachel raced along a rising spiral, each arcing sensation hotter than the last. Her fingers pressed into his back, and she wanted to pull him closer, closer still, until he was inside her, as much a part of her as her soul.

Her climax burst through her like a shaft of light, filling every nerve ending, washing over her in a flood of pleasure. Then another wave followed, a higher crest that shook her to her core. She'd barely recovered when another swell of delight shivered through her, leaving in its wake a fine trembling all over her body.

Jack held her tight against him, a lifeline for her scrambled senses. She knew intellectually what had just happened, but still she was stunned, thunderstruck by the intensity. Her breathing was still ragged, her heartbeat erratic, and if she'd been asked to stand, she would have fallen.

Rachel had to try three times to force a sound from her throat. "Oh, my," was all she managed.

She could sense him smiling against her throat. "Oh, my, indeed," he said.

She shifted her nerveless body against him. "There's something more to this, isn't there?" she asked with a smile.

"I hope so," Jack said. His hand stroked down to her derriere again and he snugged her against him. "If you're ready."

Emboldened by her recent liberation, she gave into the temptation that had driven her from the beginning. Gliding her hand down his back, she found the waistband of his briefs and explored the barrier. She slid one finger under the snug elastic, then slowly brought it around to the front, enjoying Jack's tremors as she touched his moist tip.

She could feel the growing tension in his body, his ragged breathing. She hesitated.

"I want to touch you," she whispered.

"Please," he rasped out, "do."

She trembled as she closed her hand over his erect manhood. He seemed impossibly hot, harder than she'd expected. Her tentative touches grew bolder as she let her instincts take over. The sensation of her palm against his length sent a jolt of sensation up her arm that lanced straight to her center.

He grabbed her wrist, tugged her hand gently away. "If you keep that up," he forced out, "I will lose control."

Rachel smiled, smug in her power over him. "Then come to me," she whispered.

He urged her onto her back and tugged the black lace panties off her. He quickly shed his own briefs, then lay down beside her. Nudging her legs apart with his knee, he settled in the cradle of her thighs.

She felt his manhood pressing against the center of her. She ached to have him fill her, but he hesitated.

"This might hurt," he said, the tendons in his arms ropy with tension.

"I want you," she told him, "now."

He grinned. "I aim to please."

Moving slowly, he pushed inside her. There was pain, an achy, stretchy kind of soreness. But then he slid fully inside and the rush of sensation swallowed the pain.

"Oh," she breathed softly in appreciation.

He stilled. "Are you okay?"

"Incredible," she said.

He smiled. "Then you wouldn't mind my continuing?"

"I would mind if you didn't."

Jack began to move again, and each thrust

sent her a little closer to the ultimate pleasure once more. Her hands stirred restlessly on his body, fluttering over his back, tangling in his hair, cupping his hips. She wanted him closer and she tugged at him, impatient that his powerful arms held him away from her.

"I'm too heavy for you," he said.

"I don't care," she told him, pulling against him.

Finally he settled himself down and she reveled in the feel of his body along every inch of hers. She raised her head to kiss him, tasted the dampness along his jaw, pressed her cheek against his rough one.

The spiral caught Rachel by surprise again, the mix of his taste and touch and scent roiling inside her. The world centered in the man she held in her arms, in the feelings he created in her, in her love for him. With each stroke of his body she rose higher, higher. Then one final thrust pushed her past the barrier and tumbling into ecstasy.

A moment later she heard his low moan, her whispered name, and Jack followed her with his own climax. In that bright, endless moment, they simply held each other, shudders coursing through their bodies in reaction.

Then the world settled around them again. Rachel let her eyes drift open. She nuzzled her head against Jack's, enjoying the delicious weight of his body.

Her love for Jack filled her, spilled from her. She could no more keep it locked away in her heart than she could strike the moon from the sky. She had to tell him how she felt, had to hope that her love was enough to encompass them both.

"Jack," she said softly, her hands tensing on his shoulders.

"I must be suffocating you," he said, sliding from her to lay beside her.

"No, you weren't." She raised herself on her elbow, and ran her free hand down his arm. "I have to tell you . . ."

He sensed it; she could see in the immediate tension in his face. She forged on.

"I love you, Jack." She let him absorb the simple words, then she repeated, "I love you."

Rachel saw his jaw work, anger and regret playing across his face. "You don't," he stated flatly.

She wanted to punch him. "I darn well do."

He tugged away from her and sat on the far edge of the bed, his back to her. His broad back might as well be a brick wall planted between them. It was as stiff and unyielding, as cold to her heart as any edifice.

"It doesn't matter," he rasped out. "I don't love you."

Rachel squeezed her eyes shut against the tears that threatened. She grit her teeth against the pain. "I think you do," she bit out.

He nearly turned toward her at that; she could see the brief motion before he cut it short. "You're wrong." Then he rose from the bed and without once looking at her gathered up his clothes.

As he marched off to his own room, Rachel scrambled for something more to say, some way to convince him. But she couldn't frame a single thought before he disappeared through the connecting door and banged it shut.

She heard him stomping around the room, heard the sound of some object thrown against the wall, then another slam. When she heard the sound of his feet down the hall, she realized he'd left his room.

Rachel sat up, huddling into herself. What should she do now? Call Beulah and Bonnie and ask their advice? She winced; she must be desperate if she was considering counsel from her flighty sisters. Look what their last solution had got her into.

She heard the distant ringing of a telephone and realized it must be Jack's room. She half-rose to answer it before she remembered he'd closed the connecting door. The ringing stopped, then moments later her own phone rang, nearly driving her heart straight from her chest.

"Hello?" she said into the phone.

"Rachel?" Henry Hanford's voice boomed in the receiver. "Do you know where my son's gone off to?"

A sudden tightness gripped Rachel's throat. "No." She dragged in a shuddering breath. "He just left."

A pause, then Henry said, "Are you crying?"

"No," she sobbed, tears spilling in earnest down her cheeks.

"What did he do to you?" Henry barked into the phone.

"N-nothing," Rachel said. "Only . . . only . . . he doesn't love me." The words poured out on a fresh round of tears.

Henry growled some expletive under his breath. "Do you love that worthless son of mine?"

"Y-yes, I do," she wailed.

"Then part of the plan damn well worked," he muttered. When Rachel started to ask what he meant, he continued, "Listen to me. This is what I want you to do. Can you be packed and ready in thirty minutes?"

Rachel's gaze fell on her as-yet-unpacked suitcase. "I can be ready in ten."

"Good. I'll have a car for you in twenty minutes."

Rachel rose and kicked aside the merry widow and lacy panties. She shucked the drooping hose from her legs. "Where am I going?"

"Home," he told her. "Just go home. And leave the rest to me."

Hands resting on her sewing machine table, Rachel gazed out the window at the fluffy white blossoms on her apricot tree. As the branches danced in the early afternoon breeze, the fragile petals drifted like snowfall onto the lawn.

She tried to focus on the half-finished evening dress spread across her sewing table. But in the last hour, she'd found the clock much more interesting. It was nearly two; in eighteen more minutes, Henry Hanford would arrive.

And according to Henry, Jack would turn up soon after.

She felt the familiar ache in her heart, thinking of Jack. It had only been a week since she'd left the hotel, but each day had been an agony. And since Henry's car had come for her before Jack had returned, she hadn't even been able to say good-bye to him.

But Henry had insisted Jack would be here today. Rachel knew Henry had something up his sleeve, something to do with her and Jack, but she didn't know what. She wouldn't allow herself to hope for anything more than one last chance to see Jack.

The sound of the doorbell and her sisters' chatter as they answered it sent her heart beating triple time. She flicked another glance at the clock. Ten minutes to two; Henry was early.

Rachel rose from the sewing table and batted away bits of fabric scraps from her pale blue denims. She looked down at the faded red camp shirt and dithered over whether to change before she went down. She decided she would go greet Henry, then run upstairs to change before Jack arrived.

She hurried out of her sewing room to the top of the stairs. The booming voice from below stopped her in her tracks.

Jack!

"Where is he?" he shouted.

He reached the foot of the stairs and caught her staring at him like a terrified deer. He came toward her, taking the stairs two at a time. "Where is that reprobate father of mine?"

Rachel blinked at the force of his anger. "He isn't here yet."

Jack continued up the stairs, moving like a panther until he stopped two steps below her. Eye level with her now, he gripped the rail and glared at her.

"I won't let him," he told her, one finger stabbing the air between them. "I won't let him do it."

"Do what?" Rachel asked, but the question was drowned out by the doorbell and her sisters' clamoring voices.

At the sound of his father's voice, Jack spun on the stairs and marched back down. "You!" he shouted. "You dirty-minded old man!"

Rachel followed more slowly, wondering what the heck was going on. "Glad to see you, too, Jack," Henry Hanford said jovially.

A woman followed Henry into the house, her brown hair sprinkled with gray, the glitter of humor in her dark eyes. Jack rounded on the woman.

"Moira, how can you let him do this?" he snarled.

"Your father's a grown man," she said, then turned to smile at Rachel as she reached the bottom of the stairs. "I'm Moira McFee. You must be Rachel."

Rachel shook the woman's hand as she tried to catch Henry's eye. Henry closed the distance between them and gave her a big hug. "So glad to see you again, my dear."

She glanced at Jack over Henry's shoulder. Vesuvius had nothing on him for explosiveness. He looked as if he might just blow his top in her foyer.

Rachel stepped back from Henry's embrace. "So what is it Moira's supposed to keep you from doing?" she asked the older man.

Henry beamed. "From marrying you."

"Marrying —" Rachel nearly choked on the word "— me?"

Henry gave her a long, exaggerated wink. Behind him, Jack bubbled just short of eruption.

"Oh, right," she said, going along. "We're getting married." She turned to Jack with a bright smile. "Your father proposed right after . . . right after . . ."

"She returned home," Henry finished for her.

"You can't," Jack rasped, staring at her. "You can't marry him."

Rachel stepped around Henry, chin lifted. "Why not?"

"Because you don't love him," Jack told her.

She shrugged. "I can learn to."

Jack moved closer, towered over her. "Because you love me."

A tremble of weakness washed through her, but she steeled herself against it. "Your father asked," she said, spearing him with her gaze.

He stepped nearer, so that she could feel his heat, could feel the curl of his breath stirring her hair. He reached for her, cupped his hands over her shoulders.

His gaze locked with hers. "Because I love you." It took a moment for the words to soak in, then joy burst inside her. "What did you say?" she asked softly, wanting to hear the words again.

"I love you," he repeated. "I love you and I want you to marry me."

"Yes," she whispered.

He looked stunned. "Yes?"

"Yes," she said again. "I'll marry you. Oh, Jack, I love you so."

He grinned, then caught her up in his arms. He kissed her, his mouth covering hers in a drugging assault. She clung to him like a lifeline, tasting him, loving him all over again.

The sound of Henry clearing his throat

dragged her attention back to their avid audience. Her sisters were grinning from ear to ear and Moira smiled at her fondly.

Rachel stepped back from Jack a bit, although he wouldn't let her go far. He kept his eyes on her as he told his father, "She's mine. You damn well can't have her."

Rachel peeked around Jack at Henry. He winked again. "In that case," he said, "I have an announcement to make."

Jack turned so that he could see his father. "What?"

Henry beamed a smile at Moira. The older woman fairly glowed. "Moira and I are getting married," Henry said.

Jack's jaw dropped as he stared at his father. Then a rumble started in his chest and burst into loud laughter.

"You old scoundrel," Jack said. "You never intended to marry Rachel."

Henry shook his head. He slipped an arm around Moira's shoulders and pulled her closer to him.

"My plan all along was to get you two together," Henry said.

"So the Mr. Pancake costume," Jack said, "the handcuffs, the kiss at the taping —"

"All part of my master plan," Henry acknowledged.

"And that was you in that photo of Mr.

Willens, wasn't it?" Rachel asked. "The Willenses were in on it, too."

Henry grinned and nodded. Jack gave his father a stern look. "This is the last of your meddling, old man," he said. "We decide when to give you grandkids."

Henry's eyes widened in innocence as if the thought of grandchildren had never crossed his mind. Rachel smiled at Jack's incorrigible father, a warmth spreading inside her at the thought of carrying Jack's baby.

Then Jack reached for his dad, drawing him into a hug. "Thank you, Dad," he said. "For opening my eyes to my own stupidity."

Jack pulled away and turned to Rachel. "And thank you," he said softly.

She gazed up at him with all the love in her heart. "For what?"

"For loving me," he told her.

"Always," she assured him, and with joy she looked forward to forever in his arms.